EGG HUNT

TWISTED HOLIDAYS

USA TODAY BESTSELLING AUTHOR
M.L. PHILPITT

Egg Hunt (Twisted Holidays)
Copyright © 2025 by M.L. Philpitt

This is a work of fiction. Names, characters, organizations, places, events, and incidents are products of the author's imagination or used fictitiously. Any resemblance to actual events, locations, persons living or dead are entirely coincidental.

Warning: This book contains mature content. Reader discretion is advised.

Cover Design: Dee Garcia, Black Widow Designs
Editing: Lauren, The Eclectic Editor & Rebecca Barney, Fairest Reviews Editing Services
Formatting: M.L. Philpitt

AUTHOR'S NOTE

Egg Hunt is book 2 of Twisted Holidays, a series of standalone holiday romance novellas. They can be enjoyed in any order and will have no crossover between the characters/plots.

While the series is intended to be dark romances, Egg Hunt is a shade of grey. <u>It is not dark, but does contain dark themes</u>. Jace and Payton were determined to tell the story one way, no matter how much I tried to veer another.

This book has content some people may find triggering. You can read the content warning list on the last page.

This book uses Canadian spelling. This means words will have U's in them, "re", or double LL's. (colour vs color, centre vs center, signalling vs signaling, etc.) These are not typos.

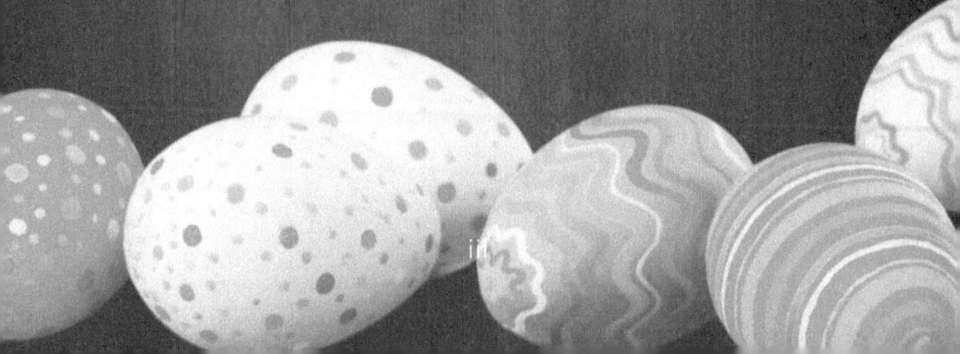

PLAYLIST

"Granite" by Sleep Token
"Face to Face" by Citizen Soldier
"Cravin'" by Stileto & Kendyle Paige
"Animal" by Chase Holfelder
"Church" by Chase Atlantic
"RUNRUNRUN" by Dutch Melrose
"Flesh" by Simon Curtis
"obsessed" by Zandros & Limi
"Morally Grey" by April Jai & Nation Haven
"touchin' me" by Chandler Leighton

*For the romance readers wanting a special kind of egg hunt.
The kind where you're chased by a masked man.*

Don't run fast enough, and you'll be caught, put to your knees, and fucked within an inch of your life.

Run, little reader, run. Jace is coming...

SIN.

The dictionary defines the term as an immoral act that goes against divine law.

There's so much wrong with that definition, so many incorrect ways it could be taken. It's staggering how no one's redefined it—not to mention the potential for religious debate around the concept of divine law being real.

The definition is pointless; sin and immorality are concepts people use to place other's actions, behaviours, appearances, and preferences into categories, nothing more. Neat little boxes to shelve or open, to store and hide away or unlock and embrace what's inside.

There is no such thing as sin. It only means someone out there has laid judgement on another. It's different for everyone. What some find wrong, others embrace. What's considered sinful for some is fun for others.

Fucked up is what it actually is.

Take the scene around me: packed bar full of rowdy patrons and drunken shrieks, pool balls being smacked across tables, and endless flirting and near-fucking happening on more than one surface is the exact picture that'd have the pearl-clutchers of this town fainting before running off to church and praying for forgiveness for daring to look upon such acts.

Get fucking real.

All this only days before the Easter holidays, when half these people will attend the church down the road, dragged there by their families and predefined notions of what they *should* be doing, where they'll celebrate the rebirth of a man who guides them in all sorts of beliefs—sin being one. They'll pray, seeking forgiveness for the shit they see as immoral—their "sins" and the consequences from them.

Yeah. Whatever.

The next day, they'll be back to doing whatever they want because what people say, believe, and do are often three different things.

"Hey, you never answered me earlier." Brad's voice cuts into my wandering thoughts. "Claire wants to know if you're coming for Easter dinner this weekend. She's trying to make it a thing, even though we've never celebrated in our lives. Prep for family life and all that."

I fucking hate the holiday, for many reasons, the true meaning behind Easter—the religious beliefs—aside. It's boring, and the town goes all out. Thankfully, this bar hasn't been subjected to the cheap Easter decorations that have thrown up all over every other business.

Normally, I stay home with a beer and pretend none of this exists, making my own judgements from afar and imagining all the things I *could* be doing that'd have the old ladies in church nicknaming me the devil.

We all have pleasures to embrace, not run from. Although, running is certainly half the fun... My idea of entertainment is hard to come by in this town, where women don't know how to keep their mouths shut.

Brad, my best friend since high school, stares at me hopefully. It's enough to make me sigh because, knowing Claire, she put him up to this, and pissing off pregnant women isn't my forte.

"Sure. Thank her for the invite. Should she be cooking in her condition, though?"

He lifts his hands, palms out, while maintaining his hold on his beer. "Hey, I said the same, and it didn't go well. She's determined. Also, 'only five months along and not an invalid.' Her words."

I finish the final swig of my third beer before resting the bottle on the nearest high-top and turning to line up my shot. A wave of dizziness passes over my eyes, forcing me to blink a few times to regain focus as I lower the pool stick onto the table.

"You miss, and the next round's on you."

Considering it's taking some serious focus to separate solids from stripes, missing is very likely to happen. When I finally make out a blue-and-white one positioned by the corner, it should be easy enough to sink, so I maneuver around the table to line up the shot.

As I send the cue forwards, a boisterous laugh from the pool table beside us throws me off-kilter, sending the ball in the wrong direction and missing the pocket, much to Brad's delight. He immediately flags down the waitress to bring us more beers.

"Fucking asshole." I eye the group of four setting up at the next table, recognizing them as guys from high school who never grew up and left, hanging around town on their parents' dime. They're the kind of people who think they're hot shit, but get them into the real world, and it'd chew them up and spit them out.

"Man, it's fuckin' good to be back. I mean, Payton—"

Payton. Nah, I must be drunker than believed if I'm hearing her name. Payton fucked off out of town the month after graduation and never looked back, cutting all contact with everyone—me included. Even her social media updates dwindled in the eight years that have passed.

She was the teenage crush I always knew would leave me behind. The friend who was not really a friend, though we ran in the same circles. The girl I grew up down the street from, attending every stage of school right from five-years-old. The one I always wanted to be mine, but knew she had plans I'd never be included in.

Not that she knew any of what I felt.

The voice who mentioned her name continues talking, the grating of it bringing me right to the past, when I wanted to punch him every day he put his hands on her. I peek toward the table, seeing fuckface—I mean, Aaron Bennett—with his old group of friends, looking every bit as smug now as he was back then.

Bennett's a self-entitled prick who thrives off his mayor daddy's money, police chief uncle's leeway, and has zero concept of hard work. In school, he was full of it, and afterwards became insufferable. Thankfully, he moved away days before I did. Where he went, I only learned after one of Payton's social media updates, in which they announced they were dating again.

They were on and off constantly, being more off than on, and things often ended with Payton crying. Fucking despised him for every tear she shed, but she never let me say anything bad before defending him.

"Hey." Brad snaps his fingers. "You okay? It's your turn. You kinda spaced."

"When did he get back?" I jerk my chin at Aaron. He should be living it up with Payton, not standing in a bar in his hometown. Although, if he's here, maybe she is as well.

Brad follows my gaze over to the next table before his own eyes roll. "Last week. I told you that the other day, but it's not like you listen to anything I say. He came back after he and Payton split." He shrugs, sipping from his fresh beer that must have been delivered when I was zoned out. "I don't really track town gossip, but he's claiming they weren't right for one another."

I tear my attention from Aaron, who's losing his game. "What'd he actually say?" Aaron isn't exactly the type to use big, respectable words like *not right for one another.*

Brad grimaces, his discomfort obvious. "That she's frigid. She cheated on him. The sex sucked. It's the polite version, anyway. Please don't make me use the exact words."

How can a person be frigid and seek sex beyond the relationship? Bennett's a special breed of moron. I could only imagine the exact words he used, but won't but won't for my own sanity.

"She's back, you know."

"Who is?"

Don't say Payton. She's not back. Her dreams took her away—rightfully so. She was attending school for veterinary medicine, and I imagine she's working in the field by now.

"Payton, obviously. You sure you're okay?"

I'm not. Not at all. And should drown myself in my freshly delivered beer.

"Why?" If she and Bennett split, why are they both home?

He shrugs. "I don't exactly talk to her, and from what I've heard, she isn't interested in talking to others either. Heard she came back to town two weeks ago, a bit before Aaron, and is working at Fawn's. Haven't seen her around, though. I'm assuming she's living in her parents' house. You know, the one they bought on the edge of town after she left but didn't sell when they retired."

A diner? She returned to work at a diner and live in her parents' cabin? That makes no sense.

"You didn't think to tell me sooner?" I hiss, my bottle thumping on the pool table's edge. "You told me about fuckface, apparently, but not her?"

"Slipped my mind. You know how stressed I've been with Claire's pregnancy. Your old crush wasn't my priority." He runs a hand through his shoulder-length hair. "Plus, you've been busy planning for the next few builds, so I figured you shouldn't be distracted. I knew this is how you'd react."

"I'm not reacting."

Bennett and his friends laugh again, almost knocking a pitcher off a table, much to the annoyance of people nearby. They have no concept of space, stumbling around one another. I eye the bouncer beside the door, hoping they'll be kicked out soon.

"You're reacting." Whatever else Brad's about to say is cut off by the sound of Payton's name coming from the asshole's mouth. His speech is more slurred than before, the five empty shot glasses in front of him probably having something to do with that.

"She was wild, guys, fuckin' wild. Sick, though. Like in the head. Wanted things I couldn't—wouldn't... Girl's fucked up. For her birthday, wanted me to chase her."

Fuck. Me. I better not have heard what I think I did.

It's amazing what alcohol can do to a person. How it loosens their lips, revealing their lies. It was never the case of Payton not being enough for him, but of *him* not giving *her* what she needs.

Fuckface is a fucking idiot. If I had the chance to call Payton Thorne mine, I'd never let her go. Not now, and not in the past.

Payton has cravings left unsatisfied, and if she's home... Maybe this Easter I can revive an old game, one only ever played once since returning from my brief stint living in Calgary.

Brad stares at me. "Whatever you're thinking, it's probably a bad idea. Not smart to get involved with a girl who recently ended a relationship with a guy who's also mysteriously returned home. There's a story there you probably shouldn't get into."

"No one said anything about getting involved. Two old friends can't meet up and chat?" I rack my pool cue even though we've yet to finish the round.

He sighs, hanging his cue beside mine before following me toward the exit. "You've always lost your mind over this girl, Jace. I just want to make sure you don't again, especially when you have no idea what's going on."

My mind's already lost from what Bennett was saying, every thought shifting to her.

I break away from him in the parking lot, heading in the opposite direction of my parked truck. "I'm walking home. Too drunk to drive."

He thumbs toward his SUV, a trade-in from the beat-up truck he used to own before last month, another step in preparing for the birth of his child. "I can drive you."

"It's fine." I wave him away and begin my way to a small, cabin-style home on the very edge of town, fenced by a vast forest with so many possibilities.

I have to see her. To see she's *here*, like Brad claims. To know she's alright, even if from afar.

And come up with a plan to speak with her.

TWO
PAYTON

HOME *SHOULD* BE a sweet slice of heaven, except the cabin my parents bought right before retirement doesn't feel like it.

Everything about this place, this town—a village, really—feels so different, despite it being the place I was born and raised. Before eight years ago, every memory I have is within these streets. Perhaps it's because that girl—the one who moved away at eighteen, hooked back up with her unsteady high school boyfriend like an idiot seeking a happily-ever-after with the constant in her life (despite the few breakups), then had life bitch-slap her in the face—is not the woman who's returned.

Maybe it's because, as a kid, I never had to experience the assholes running this place and how they only take one another's side.

The door slams behind me, rattling this old house that, for some grand reason, my parents decided to buy after I left. Then, only two years later, they decided they hated living by the woods—despite it being what they initially wanted for retirement—and relocated all the way to Prince Edward Island to "get away from everything." Whatever that means.

I'm actually lucky they didn't sell because it became my saving grace when I couldn't afford the rent on my Toronto apartment and coming home became my best option. Having credit card debt taller than the trees outside means needing to save every dollar possible to restart, and the prices of Toronto weren't making it feasible. Here, I get the chance to begin again and claim the life I should have had, rather than the fuckery it became.

Or, hoped to, anyway. Instead, I cross the room and slam three notes onto the coffee table with as much impact as paper is able to make. The messy handwriting taunts me. The newest note, found this morning before leaving for my shift at Fawn's Diner, is on top.

YOU'VE ALWAYS WANTED TO BE CHASED. WHY ISN'T THIS ENOUGH?

It's unsigned, but it's from Aaron. After eight years together, his writing is as familiar as my own, as is the disdain his pen pressed into each word. It's become the third in two weeks—a fact only I find remotely concerning, apparently.

Should have figured that's how it'd go when I took them all to the local police station, only to have them dismissed because Aaron's fucking *uncle* is the chief. Coupled with his father being the mayor, Aaron can do no wrong in any of these people's eyes.

I spread the three notes apart.

The second, received last week:

COME BACK TO ME OR PAY THE PRICE.

The first, received four days after arriving:

YOU'VE RUN RIGHT INTO MY TRAP.

Not the most creative guy. Still, my stomach twists, and I shove the papers away before fear can take hold. Aaron's harmless, but taunting, almost-threats are new for him, so nothing's certain.

With a weary sigh and throbbing feet from a long day at the diner, I kick off my shoes, already anticipating a hot bath to ease the swelling. In there, I'll pretend to *not* be tempted to drown myself.

I'm not suicidal, but fuck if everything happening won't soon drive me to it. Unfortunately, his half-assed threats aren't even the beginning; they're the cherry on top of a fucked-up situation.

Having next to no options meant moving home was my best one. Aaron made sure of that, and some-fucking-how—because the world is that cruel—he also came back two days after me, into a house on the opposite end of town, bought and paid for by his rich parents. He was the popular one in school, and maybe he's chasing that high again. Or he's followed me...a possibility by the notes he's been leaving.

"Maybe he'll get so stoned one day, he'll fall off a mountain," I grumble, forcing myself to my feet and wearily making my way to the kitchen.

Supper. Bath. Bed.

Then tomorrow: repeat everything I did today.

Day after: everything again.

And so on until I make enough to pay everything off and decide what's next.

After two bites into a sandwich I quickly threw together, my phone rings. There's only four people who'd be calling. By process of elimination, it shouldn't be my boss, considering she'd be thick in the supper rush by now, and it won't be my parents due to time zone differences, which leaves Gwen.

"Hey," I mumble around a bite of food after tapping the button to answer the call. "What's up?"

"You working this weekend?"

"Friday, yeah. Not Saturday through to Monday. Diner's closed, sadly." Normally, businesses would be closed for Good Friday and open Saturday, which is no actual holiday, but Fawn and Jim have their grandkids visiting, so they've opted to swap the days around to maximize the time they'll spend with them.

"Sadly." She snorts. "P, you're probably the only person who's upset about being off for the holiday."

Yeah, well, try working through a mountain of debt where every dollar earned counts.

I grunt. "Eh. Why do you ask?"

"Because we can hang out for the holiday. Maybe on Sunday?"

"I don't celebrate Easter."

"Neither do I, but there's a first time for everything."

I groan at the idea. Considering Gwen's the only person around my age to embrace my return, and we haven't hung out much outside of the diner, I'd be a bitch to turn her down. She's my only friend, because my old ones either moved away or took Aaron's side because he got to spread his version of the story first: poor girl cheated on the golden boy. It was a fable he wrote to push me out of existence. It should hurt, but I expected nothing less from Aaron. By the time I arrived, even though I made it to town before him, I'd already been branded a few different colourful titles—bitch, whore, and frigid being some of the nicer ones. As though any of them had stakes in *our* drama. Small towns suck that way.

But Gwen isn't from here. Pretty sure she's certifiably insane, because she's one of those people who *chose* to live here, relocating here a few years ago while chasing a small-town vibe that reminded her of the show *Gilmore Girls.*

"Fine," I agree, trying to tamper down on the unwillingness. "Nothing major, though."

"Sure, sure. I'll figure something out." Through the phone, I can almost hear the way her mind starts racing at highway speeds. She's about to make hanging out a big thing.

"Good day at work?"

"Kids will be kids." Gwen's a private nanny to a family with three children under five. "You?"

"Slow. Thankfully, no drop-ins from the dick." I eye the notes again, wondering if I should mention them. I didn't bother with the first two, because I assumed they were Aaron being an ass, but three might be saying something else. Which is why courage took hold long enough this morning for me to seek help—even if that ended before it began.

"You can't let him bother you, P. He's doing that shit on purpose." Her advice is nothing I'm not already aware of, but it's impossible to ignore Aaron's constant presence and written taunts. "You know what? We need to find you a man."

"Uh, no." I lower my plate into the sink, deciding to make washing it tomorrow's problem, and leave the kitchen. "A man is what started this mess. I need to stay away from them."

"They're not all bad. Besides, it's only sex. Hook up, forget about the loser, and go from there."

"In this town?" After a final check of my front door to ensure it's locked, I tread down the hallway toward my bedroom, stopping by the bathroom first to begin running my bath water. "Have you seen the people who live here? The only guys our age are Aaron's friends, and they're a definite no." More like a *fuck no*.

"You're hooking up, not marrying the guy. Maybe fucking one of his friends *is* what's needed. Create some drama in his life." Gwen's tone does nothing to mask her dislike of Aaron. "There's seriously not one guy you'd fuck?"

There was one. Maybe. One I never crossed the line with because we were never that close. I stupidly continued running back to Aaron like a dog with a bone; he was popular and good looking, and my seventeen-year-old hormonal brain believed he was right for us. In hindsight, the best may have actually been the non-friend (because we were kidding ourselves about claiming to only be classmates) I had.

Last I saw online, he, too, moved away a few years ago. Although I've looked since being home, he hasn't been around town. And I'm not brave enough to ask anyone about him.

"Not anymore," I finally reply.

"We'll find someone," she says with certainty, like it's that easy. "Even if we have to keep driving 'til we do."

"You're oddly invested in my sex life." I laugh, entering my bedroom. "Like, weirdly so, but I'm gonna let you go now since my bath is nearly filling."

"Alright, enjoy. If you have a waterproof vibrator, bring that with you."

"Hanging up now."

Still laughing, I toss my cell onto the bed and undress, ignoring the fact I *do* have a waterproof vibrator hidden in my bedside table. It's been there since I unpacked but has never touched, because work keeps me too tired. Most nights, I pass out as soon as my head hits the pillow.

I head for the bathroom, eager to slide into the hot water and let it wipe everything else away. It prickles at my sore feet as I step in, and relaxes my back when I fully sink below the surface. Leaning over, I grab the horror novel read only during bath time, then settle back for a bone-chilling story about a serial killer targeting blonde women.

AN HOUR OR SO LATER, when my feet are no longer sore, my body is pruning, and the water is cooling, I drain the tub and wrap myself in a clean, fluffy towel from a shelf by the tub before heading to my room.

As I pass the window in my room, a strange sensation settles over me—one that slows my steps when they should be quickening, simultaneously churning my stomach and warming me. It's an urge to carefully scan my surroundings, as if I'm being watched, except I'm safe in my own home.

Aren't I?

While I should be bolting to dress in something less revealing than a towel in case I'm not alone, I instead lean closer to the window, scanning the dark outdoors. There are no streetlights behind the house, so everything is black. No matter how much I scan, the only shapes visible, with help from the moonlight, are the distinct trees of the endless forest that stretches so far, it eventually reaches the next town's boundaries.

Maybe it's in my head. Wouldn't be the first time I've felt like this. I push off the window with a shake of my head, hoping water merely slipped through my ears and into my brain, making me senseless. Still, I slide the curtains shut, just in case, and get dressed before slipping into bed.

Even as I settle, my attention remains on the window. Few people know where I'm staying. Considering Aaron's been leaving notes, he knows, but sulking around at nighttime? That'd involve getting off his ass past five p.m., which would be a first.

Still, I tug the blanket high over my shoulders to hide.

JACE

ONCE SLEEP CLEARS from my head, I reach for my phone.

ME

I'm grabbing coffee before heading to the jobsite. Want anything?

BRAD

You're setting yourself up.

ME

How so? I'm buying caffeine before a long day of smacking a hammer against wood. Something wrong with that?

BRAD

You know exactly what, don't act dumb. It's a messy situation. Leave it.

Good thing I enjoy messy.

My phone vibrates with Brad's final message.

BRAD

And yes, I'll take coffee.

He can never go long without caffeine. Truthfully, even if he said no, he'll be getting one so no one has to deal with his cranky, caffeine-deprived ass.

I throw on jeans and a plain black tee, with a flannel shirt overtop to counter the mid-April chill that sometimes still lingers, before donning a faded black cap with my company's logo practically peeling from it. By the door, I slip into construction boots that track a bit of extra dirt than normal.

Dirt from the woods behind Payton's house, where I watched and waited last night until catching sight of her. After an hour of standing there, she appeared wrapped in a towel that sat high on her thigh, giving me a tantalizing peek of skin. With the distance, I knew she couldn't see me. Unfortunately, there wasn't much of her I could make out either, which only added to my eagerness to get to Fawn's and see her in person for the first time in eight years.

She was looking for me. Somehow, she knew. Her head turned every so often, searching. I wished I could have seen her eyes—a vibrant combination of blue and grey, like a rainstorm in the evening—filled with delicious fear. I craved to witness the way she gripped her towel tighter and shifted from foot to foot.

Payton's fear...fuck, that'd be nirvana.

Her social media hasn't been updated in years, so getting to see her up close has me finishing getting ready quickly, grabbing my phone and keys, and heading outside to my truck.

She was beautiful back then, and the limited view I got last night showed she's still just as gorgeous, if not more. She looks good. Healthy. She actually has hips to grab on to, ones that won't make me afraid I'll accidentally snap her in two.

I leave the house a bit earlier than normal, knowing I'm not about to rush this interaction. Being the boss means I shouldn't be late to the jobsite, but I don't make a habit of it. Besides, we've only just begun working on our latest contract now; since the winter frost is mostly gone, we're finally able to dig into the ground. Work's been steady for the company, often hired for jobs in towns a few hours on either side of us. For this one, we're building a new neighbourhood in the next town over.

I drive my beat-up truck a few streets over to the diner that's been open since before my birth. It's owned by an elderly couple, Fawn and Jim, who both somehow still work daily. Admittedly, it's been much too long since I've dropped by, instead getting into the habit of making coffee to go at home. If Payton's working here, though, it's about to become my daily stop again.

The metal handle on the door to Fawn's Diner is worn down from the numerous hands grabbing it, and mine is one more as I haul it open. Warmth pulls me inside, alongside the pleasant smells of freshly baked goods, coffee, and the best damn soup to exist on the planet.

There's a small hum of chatter, and I scan over the handful of people sitting in the booths: an elderly couple in the nearest one, a group in the one at the very farthest end, and a younger girl in the middle one—a student, if the laptop, textbook, and visible stress are any indication.

I stride forward, noting the cheap Easter decorations everywhere. And I mean *everywhere*. Fawn took the weekend holiday and blew it up to involve window clings on every glass pane, egg-shaped cardboard streamers hanging from random ceiling tiles, mini rabbit figurines on each table, and baskets scattered on every other free surface. It looks like a store threw up.

I scan up and down for staff, praying Payton's working today and no one else. Even if last night proved she's as real as she was years ago, it wasn't enough. To get through today, she better be here, and I better be able to talk with her.

When the door to the back swings open, my heart skips three beats and a hunger without a name, but one demanding satisfaction, ignites in my stomach.

Fuck, I won't survive her this time.

"Good morning!" she calls out, eyes averted and head low.

Her hair tumbles from her loose ponytail, strands framing her face, and her freckles are as obvious as ever. Grey eyes lift, and her next words die on her tongue as she identifies me. In the past, her stormy eyes were lightning, sparking every time I was around, but now they speak of catastrophic events—of city-destroying floods and power-cutting winds. It's pain. A pain undoubtedly put there by her asshole ex.

The sight of her after all this time shoves me off a cliff and straight into the past. For a moment, I'm not myself; I'm the kid she knew, tongue-tied in her presence.

Those fucking lips. Her face. Her body. She's all curves, the perfect turbulent wave I long to run my hands over, feeling every inch for myself. She looks fucking amazing, even better than the woman from our high school graduation. Back then, she was so thin, like she wasn't eating enough; I swear I would have broken her. Which was why, when I could, it was my mission to deposit snacks on her desk, disguising the act as a joke since I never witnessed her eating. It killed me she was starving herself, presumably for Aaron, but now she looks healthy.

One thousand percent, Aaron's a fucking idiot for letting her go. Then again, he's probably the kind of man who wants his women to kneel and obey his every whim, whereas I much prefer the fight, the excitement, the hunt. I want her to make it difficult because she craves it, not because she thinks she's doing what I expect.

She smiles, and I'm yanked right back to the halls of the small high school we attended one town over. We weren't friends per se, but were friendly, considering our lockers were beside one another for the four years we were there.

This Easter, I know what I'm praying for.

One night of sin with her.

FOUR

PAYTON

LIFE ESPECIALLY SUCKS at this moment.

Hiding in the kitchen of Fawn's isn't exactly screaming *great life*.

Today's round of fuckery comes from the group loudly chatting I was forced to wait on while ignoring their muttered comments, my grip on my poor pen a testament to the level of restraint exerted. One more comment, and I'd be bleeding blue ink when it cracked—then they'd be getting a carafe of coffee over their heads. Because waiting on Aaron and his friends isn't how I wished to start my day.

Despite the notes, he hasn't actually been around. So what makes today the day to torment me? He hasn't referenced anything, and while I debated bringing the notes up, I chickened out because *not* engaging him was the high route I opted to take.

"You okay?" Jim, the cook and co-owner, asks from where he's placing a few plates into the tray that'll soon be slid inside the industrial dishwasher.

"Yeah," I reply, but we're both aware it's a lie.

I *hate* how small Aaron makes me feel, even after the year since our break up. While I've gotten over him and mostly grew past everything he said, his actions still linger like an ever-present wound on my insides.

More than that, I despise how long it took me to get my head out of my ass and see through his bullshit. Unfortunately, all those realizations came too late to avoid the damage.

The familiar chime of the door sounds, informing me of an entering customer. With a resigned sigh, I push through the swinging door, keeping my head low and eyes averted from the table in the far right, as I greet the newcomer. Forcing cheer into my voice, I say, "Good morning!"

The newcomer hovers midway between the counter and the door, and it's with a stuttered breath my heart skips a beat. No fucking way it's him. Out of everyone whom it *could* be, I should be thrilled it's the best non-friend I've ever had.

Jace Hayes.

For some reason, I fear his opinion more than anyone else's. Perhaps because he's always been so good at *not* judging me, even when I needed a firm kick in the ass to shove me on a better path. But it's been years. I'm no longer the same person, and presumably, neither is he.

He blinks, shaking his head, and continues approaching. Realistically, toward the counter to order, but the way his large strides eat up the small space, dirty boots on the black-and-white tiled floor, makes me feel like I'm being chased. The mental images of him hunting me have my hands pinching the sides of my jeans, and I force breath through my lungs, eyes on him. *The customer*, I remind myself; only a customer to serve, same as anyone else in here. It's a struggle to keep my expression passive, yet still friendly.

Maybe he won't recognize me. It's an unlikely hope, though, because if I recognize him, surely he'll recognize me.

And, holy fuck, do I ever recognize him. Jace back then was hot—I'll admit that—but now, he's downright sexy. And huge. Seriously, where the fuck did those muscles come from? His dad owned a construction company, and it's clear from just the look of him, it's what Jace now does for a living.

He slides onto one of the stools, his frame too large for the small, red seat. Muscled arms rest on the counter, and his finger traces the stack of menus piled beside him as he lifts his head, gazing at me with eyes so impossibly dark, they're like an endless cavern I could see myself falling headfirst into. And like a cavern, they'd probably lead to my demise, because being attracted to a man isn't on my immediate radar. Been there, done that, have the debt to prove it. And creepy notes—let's not forget those.

His arms on the counter draw my attention to the way his plaid button-down is open, revealing a plain tee beneath. The sleeves are rolled up, prepared for a day of work. A baseball cap sits on his head, a black one that's a bit faded and even frayed along the beak's edge. It makes his hair, still retaining its slight curls, frame his face.

He smirks, and even the simple line of his mouth makes me flushed, like his mouth has secrets he'll never admit to but could certainly make me reveal.

"No fucking way. Payton Thorne."

Damn it. I force a smile, my lips tightly pressed together while glancing at the far corner, where Aaron and his friends still sit.

"Jace."

"You came back." There's a second question beneath the first, asking *Why?*, which I ignore.

"Two weeks ago, yeah."

"Yeah?" He smiles, showing perfectly straight teeth. Why the fuck am I thinking about this man's teeth? "Clearly, I'm shit at keeping up with local news. How long have you been working here?"

"Few days."

"Well, that'd explain it. Nice to see you again, Thorne. It's been some time."

Dark eyes scan me, making me hot in places that haven't been heated in a while. I hate what he must see—my body, my jeans not quite fitting right, my apron unable to hide the bulges that have developed over the past few years, thanks to stress eating while living with the asshole across the room. *I* have come to appreciate my body, but Aaron never took a breath between insults; that shit weighs heavy on the mind and comes back to haunt me, even now. Especially when at the centre of someone's attention.

"What can I get you?" I ask, remembering my role as a waitress, needing the distraction of work to pull me back.

"Coffee please. Black."

Simple and sensible. I reach behind me for a white mug and the carafe before pouring it full, then sliding it to him. He takes a mouthful, regardless of the steam wisping from the surface, and releases a pleased growl in what might just be the most sensual sip I've ever witnessed.

"Good shit," he rumbles, setting the mug down.

"It's free refills." *If you stay long enough.* Do I want him to leave? For so long, Jace was the presence I looked forward to joking with between classes, though neither of us really acknowledged the bond being a friendship.

"Heard you were living in Toronto. How was that?"

He's asking why I've come back without outright saying the words. I appreciate that. People are too nosy for their own good, and anyone else wouldn't beat around the question.

My gaze flicks to Aaron in the corner, who's talking with his hands. "I'm sure you've heard the stories."

Jace tracks my attention, a shadow passing over his expression. "I've heard *a* story, yeah, but I want yours."

"Does it matter?" I busy myself by retrieving a damp cloth and wiping the stretch of counter farther away from him. It's not dirty, but it's enough to distract me from tumbling into old desires and setting myself up for failure. "My side, his side—it's all true in one form or the other. My perspective is only mine."

When I pass by him to go to the opposite end of the counter, he stops me with a hand on my wrist. His fingers are warm, wrapping me in a hold I already know would be impossible to escape from even without attempting.

"Then make it mine too," he rasps in a low voice. "Because I know for damn sure you cheating on him was a lie the coward made up to take the heat off himself. I knew you well enough, Payton. You weren't that girl, and I don't believe you're that woman either."

I open my mouth to reply. With what, I'm not certain. The truth, maybe, or at least some of it, because it feels nice not to be blamed. Especially after my experience with the police not believing me. Whatever my response would be is cut off by an obnoxious shout.

"Waitress! I need more coffee."

My teeth jam into my tongue and, for a full three seconds, I don't budge. I'd rather dig my own grave at this point than have a repeat of earlier, especially now with Jace witnessing. My hatred is tamped by reminders of *why* I'm doing this, and I snatch the carafe. Without a glance at Jace, who's probably judging me, I exit the safety of the counter and cross toward Aaron and his friends—all of whom know my name, making the use of my job title downright rude.

The one closest to me holds up his mug without looking, and I focus everything onto pouring the coffee into the mug and not on them, no matter how tempting.

"Anyone else?" I ask in a lifeless voice, repeating the mantra of *"do it for the money"* over and over in my head while praying they release me from this torture session and allow me to escape into the back room.

"Yeah, me." It's the bane of my existence. Unlike his friend, he doesn't hold up his mug. I'm okay with it, though, because the asshole probably wouldn't keep it steady.

As I reach across the table for his mug, I feel like the entire diner is watching, even though it's probably just my anxiety making the back of my neck tingle.

I straighten, and his hand snatches my wrist to pin me close, pinching the skin painfully. He sits upright, glaring to discourage me from making a scene, and ensures his voice carries no further than the group when muttering, "Playing this game is cute, baby, but you'll come crawling back. You always do. This time will be no different."

Crawling across coals after having my legs sawed off would be more preferable.

I yank my wrist away, ready to make a scene if he doesn't release me, but satisfied when he does. "The only game here is the notes you continue leaving on my porch. Isn't that what they are—your pitiful attempts to scare me back to you? It'll never work, so give up."

A flicker of surprise cracks his smirk, neither of us expecting those words to come from my mouth. Certainly not me, because talking about them gives life and meaning to his torment. Letting them die and feigning naïveté could be safest, at least until figuring out what his goal is.

His grin stretches wider than before—faked. "Don't know what you mean. You're delusional, believing someone would leave you love notes."

"Threats won't win me back." Nothing will. "Instead of spending all your time bullying me, get a fucking job and help pay off the debt *you* accumulated."

Aaron's gaze flicks to his friends, then back to me. "You're mine, whether you like it or not, Pay. Don't make me remind you of all the ways I own your ass."

"It's been a year," I hiss. "Fuck off." Thrilled to be done with this interaction, I muster a friendly-ish waitress smile and twist to leave, only to be stopped again by my ex's grating voice.

FIVE

JACE

WHATEVER ACTUALLY WENT DOWN between them, I *have* to know. When Payton went over to his table, her discomfort was obvious. She seemed more beaten down than I could recall her ever being, shoulders almost to her ears. Then they started speaking to one another, their tones too low for me to catch, and he fucking *touched* her. His hand on her wrist, uninvited, nearly had me over there, if not for her quick reaction when she shrugged him off.

It signals the switch inside her: gone is the spooked bunny guise and out comes the wolf. Her motions become jerky, their tones rising ever so slightly. Based on his annoyed expression and barely concealed rage, he isn't liking what she's saying. It's the concealed anger making me tense, ready to react the moment he lifts a hand to her again. Anger isn't something to joke about, especially when not reined in appropriately.

Once Payton finishes filling their mugs and pivots to return to the counter, Aaron loudly announces they need to leave. Despite the fresh drinks her job forced her to pour, they begin filing from the booth.

Dicks. But the sooner they fuck off, the sooner she'll no longer have to stress about people undeserving of her breath.

The two guys who were seated across from Aaron leave first, but not before one of them pulls a blue five-dollar bill from his wallet to pay for both drinks. At two dollars a coffee, that leaves her with a minuscule tip. Payton deserves their entire fucking credit balance after putting up with their asses.

Aaron stands, letting the fourth guy out of the booth. Once he joins the others who all exit the diner together, Aaron sneers down at Payton, saying something I don't catch. Whatever it is makes her cheeks flush, and she backs away with a glare.

As Aaron goes to leave, his arm swipes at the full mug, sending it shattering onto the floor. Shards of white ceramic scatter across the tiles, and hot liquid spills everywhere in a pool of black. Some splashes on the cuffs of Payton's jeans, and she hops back with a hiss. The diner falls deathly silent as the few other patrons observe the spectacle. It's so silent, I can practically hear the tears of frustration and anger brewing behind Payton's eyes.

Rage erupts within me. I snag the rag she was previously wiping the counter with and cross the room to shove between them, grabbing Aaron's collar without another thought. My other fist slams into his face, my punch filled with the animosity I've had for him since we were twelve-fucking-years-old, when he opened his mouth about my father's business being less respectable than his own father's as mayor. My second punch is a tribute to high school, when I was forced to witness him hurt Payton's heart time after fucking time. Years of pent-up resentment has him screeching in pain like a little bitch, not bothering to swing back.

Payton yells something that sounds like, "Stop!" She's doing what she's always done for this asshole: trying to maintain the peace. He gave her up and doesn't deserve her kindness any longer. Not that he ever really did.

I release his collar to shove the cloth into his chest, the force behind my action sending him stumbling against the table. "Clean it up, asshole."

"Fuck you, Hayes." He spits a glob of clotted blood onto the floor and rubs at his cheek, now a vibrant red, then makes the mistake of trying to go around me.

"Whoa, whoa, men, break it up or get the hell out of here!" Jim, the diner's co-owner, nudges between us, his glare heavy on us both until I drop my arm, turning to scowl at the elderly man.

"Your guests are harassing your waitress."

Weathered eyes dart to where Payton stands somewhere behind me. Given Jim's hardening expression, I can only assume she signalled to him my words are true. With pinched lips, he takes the cloth from me. "Even so, I can't have you treating this place like it's somewhere for a bar brawl. Mr. Bennett, please leave."

Aaron casts a sneer my way as he passes. "Liked that, did you? Playing the white knight?" He's gone before I can react, shouldering a hanging paper egg out of his way.

The tension in the air fizzles until an awkward silence remains, broken only by my heavy breathing and Jim asking Payton, "You okay?"

"I'm fine. I'll grab a mop." She skitters to the back room.

Jim eyes me standing amidst the mug's remains and pool of coffee. "Do I need to toss you out as well?"

"As long as the prick stays the fuck out of her way, then no."

He frowns out the window at where Aaron and his friends are stalking away. "I don't disagree, and thank you for intervening, but I can't have people causing trouble in here." He heads to the back room as Payton returns, pushing a mop bucket.

I grab it from her, and she immediately tries to steal it back. "Uh, no—"

"Go clean yourself up."

"This is my job." She reaches for the mop again, but I swing it to the side and out of her grasp.

"Your job is to serve customers, not clean up after exes who have no respect. Go on. Take a break. If anyone comes in, I'll let them know you'll be a minute."

Right now, I *dare* someone to say shit about her impromptu break.

Her behaviour of conceding is the same as in the past: two rapid blinks and a sigh. "Fine, but it's not your job either. Leave it, and I'll clean when I get back."

"Go, Payton." Finished arguing my case, I give her my back and start squeezing excess water from the mophead with the bucket.

Cleaning the spilled coffee goes quickly. I return the mop and bucket to the back room, leaving it just inside the swinging door before grabbing the broom and dustpan in the corner. Jim says nothing as I shuffle around his kitchen, gathering what I need, then returning moments later with the swept-up ceramic shards.

"That was kind of you," he says, taking the dustpan from me.

I'm heading back to my seat, where my abandoned coffee still sits, as Payton returns, her face damp and stray strands of hair sticking to her forehead. Coffee is still evident on her pants, but hopefully, it'll be a bit less uncomfortable for the remainder of her shift.

"You didn't have to do that."

"I know, but I wanted to. Someone had to stand up to him."

Her lips pinch. "That someone should have been me, not you."

"You've had years of dealing with him. Maybe it was my turn."

Her eyes flick to where my hand is wrapped around the mug, my knuckles red and splitting—injuries well worth it. They highlight the large, white scar across the back of my hand, homage to a mistake made on the job two years ago.

"I can get you something for that if you'd like."

"It's fine. I'll get more beat up at work." *Fuck, work.* I slide my cell from my jeans, checking the time. Fuck Bennett for stealing all my time with her. "I have to go, unfortunately. Bad form if the boss is late. Can I get two coffees to go please? Both black."

"Sure." She gives me her back while preparing two to-go coffees in paper cups before turning back to face me and resting them in front of me.

"What time do you get off?"

She stills, her debate practically written on her face. Her mind is racing, and no doubt her heart is as well. Hopefully, it won't be the only time I make her heart race.

"Five. Why?"

"My time with you was stolen, and it's been entirely too long, Thorne. I've missed seeing your face, and I'm not willing to go another few years without it. Before you up and move a second time without a goodbye, I want to see you again."

Her lips part, a tease of her tongue against her bottom lip making my dick twitch. She has no damn idea what she does to my sanity. "Uh, I'm not sure... I mean, I'm not—"

I end her uncertainty by resting my hand over hers. "To chat, Payton, nothing more." Yet. "Seeing you today was a fuckin' shock, that's all. I just wanna catch up. You okay with that?"

She stares for a long moment before lowering her head in a barely there nod, but I'll take it. Her skittishness is half her charm—when she's flustered and not shutting down from shitty exes. My smile is genuine as I stand and throw a red fifty on the counter, paying for my two coffees, Brad's, Aaron's because he didn't, and a decent tip for all of us.

"Have a good day, Payton. Don't take people's shit."

GENERALLY, I get really focused on work, but today...today isn't it. Five o'clock can't come fast enough.

Brad notices and trails me to my truck, where I triple check a few details on the blueprints we were given to follow.

"So..." He reaches for his coffee, now cold, resting on my open truck bed. "You saw Payton this morning."

"Yeah."

He waits a few seconds. "And?"

"And what? Her stupid ex caused trouble and intentionally knocked a fresh cup of coffee all over the floor. So I punched him. Twice."

He coughs around the plastic lid. "Man, you can't be acting like that. She can fight her own battles. She's not the girl you liked back then. You can't tell me you've spent all these years pining after her, waiting for this chance."

"Obviously not. She left to live her life, and I lived mine." We were two old acquaintances without a reason to communicate, but now that she's back, things are different. "We were friends, you know that. Now, it's two old friends hanging out."

"No." He leans over, blocking the blueprints with his hand until I'm forced to give up studying them. "I remember you were in fuckin' love with the girl, but you hid it behind that weird relationship you called friendship. The one where you acted like cats fighting all the time."

Old memories bring a smile to my face.

"Look," he sighs, drawing the word out. "Be careful. I'd hate to see you hurt when she up and leaves again. Why not start with the egg hunt this weekend? Get her to go to that."

"Hate that thing." Can't recall the last time I participated. Hunting for little ceramic eggs isn't my idea of fun.

But it does give me an idea for something else—a different kind of game I can play with Payton. One that might help her out of that shell of hers, if what Bennett said about her last night is true.

First, I'll need to get her to tell me what went down between her and Bennett without being obvious about it.

"Maybe."

After a final sip of his drink, he returns to work, and I finish examining the blueprints. My mind slips away, once again, this time to a stool across from a tentative little rabbit.

SIX

PAYTON

WHEN THE DOOR to the diner swings open with extra gusto that blows the fake Easter décor around, I know who it is without looking up. She slips onto the stool across from me as I'm placing her customary croissant on a plate and sliding it over.

Gwen takes an animated bite, groaning loudly as she chews. "Always so tasty. It's practically orgasmic."

"Clearly. Seems like you're on the verge of one. Please don't, 'cause it's not something I want to clean up."

Placing the treat down, she looks up. "Speaking of messes, heard about the one you had in here earlier. It's the buzz of the town."

Damn it.

"Exes suck." Thankfully, she doesn't linger on the topic before launching into her day with the kids she nannies for, allowing me to *hm* and *ah* where appropriate while restocking sugar containers, rolling forks and knives into napkins, and a bunch of other afternoon tasks in the slow time between lunch and dinner.

Gwen finishes her story, then swigs the mocha she ordered in the meantime. "So, what happened this morning?"

"Couldn't let that go, eh? You said it was the talk of the town, so you already know."

She rolls her eyes. "I'm nosy. Heard Jace Hayes came to your rescue. He's yummy to look at. Sin wrapped up in a sexy package."

Something twists inside me at hearing her talk about him. Something close to envy, which is ridiculous, because it's never been like that with us. Besides, getting involved with anyone while my ex is bothering me is asking for more trouble.

"We're old friends. Went to school together."

She sucks her teeth. "Hm. Yeah, so when I see old friends, I don't get on my hands and knees to clean the mess someone else made."

"He's nice, that's all." *And intense.* The years haven't lessened that intensity at all. "And he wasn't on his hands and knees. He used a mop and broom."

"Mhm. If you say so. Remember what I said last night? Maybe make him your one. We all need a bit of rebound sex."

Rebound sex with Jace? The vision makes me shiver more than it should, because the ideas don't go together in my head. Sex and Jace maybe, but it only being a rebound? Less so.

What am I saying? Nope, not the purpose of life right now.

Especially when I don't know Jace like that. I've never seen him date. And after the shit with Aaron, men aren't on my radar for a while. Not until life gets back on track.

"Now that I got you thinking about it, maybe you should invite him to the hunt Sunday afternoon?"

"The hunt?" I ask before the date hits me—despite the Easter décor puked all over this place. "They're still doing those?"

The annual egg hunt always occurring on Easter Sunday was fun as a kid. Being out all afternoon, hunting for small, ceramic eggs the members of town council hid. It's a community-wide event, but was designed mainly for the kids, giving them something to look forward to. My last one was when I was thirteen. After that, I either hid in my room as an angsty teenager or camped out at a friend's house.

"Right, forgot you grew up here. I vote dragging your ass from your house for at least one social event. That could be our weekend plans we agreed to. Maybe with Jace as your motive, you'll show up."

Jace at the Easter hunt? I'm trying to recall a time I've ever seen him at one. Maybe as a young kid, but I didn't pay attention then.

"You said so yourself, P. He's only a friend." She leans closer, pressing into the counter. "Look, I know being home wasn't on your to-do-in-life list, but I personally love that we've become friends. And if you and he were close years ago, what's the harm in reconnecting and sparking that up again?"

Because this morning, he wasn't looking at me like he wanted to be my friend.

For the sake of this conversation, I murmur, "Maybe," but instantly regret it when her face falls. I've been a shit friend to her, always hiding in my house and acting mopey during our conversations.

My gaze goes to the booth Aaron and his friends occupied this morning. It's all because of him. I don't hate this place, even if it wasn't a part of my grand plan. Gwen's made being home more acceptable, and having Jace as a friend again would be nice.

"It's Aaron," I admit quietly. "Coming back was one thing. Took swallowing a bit of pride and all, but when he followed, it brought all the shit back. *He's* the reason I'm in this mess; yet, he's acting like *I* was the villain in the relationship. I appreciate you, though, and everything you've done."

Once again, three scraps of paper come to mind, and I debate mentioning them to her. Knowing Gwen, she'd want to go after him or something when *technically* there's no proof he's even behind them. Being familiar with his handwriting is the only way I know for certain, but he could be getting a friend to leave them at my house.

"*Are* you over him?"

That's a definite yes. "I did a lot of thinking in the months following the breakup, and realized I only got back with him after grad because we'd dated before, and it seemed right. Looking back, we fought a lot. He liked to go out with friends, while I preferred staying home. Our sex life was *not* good. I'm a saver, he's a spender. The differences were too much."

So many differences, so why *would* he want me back? Cheating on me was sign number one he was done with me, so his harassment makes no sense.

"The guy's a dick."

"He is, but you're also right. Yeah, let's do the hunt. As for Jace coming...maybe."

She winks and slides off the stool before tossing a bill onto the counter. "Alrighty, let me know. And who knows, since you're new prey in town, you might be subjected to a whole other kind of hunt." She breaks off laughing at her own joke.

"What are you talking about?"

"Oh, it's this rumour floating around that, a few years ago, this guy came around at Easter time for a different kind of egg hunt, if you know what I mean." She waggles her brows, but no, I really don't know what she means. At my continuous blank expression, she sighs. "You search for eggs; he searches for you. Keep up, P. Apparently, he's real kinky and shit—likes to play this game where he picks a woman and hunts her at night. Wears a mask so it's anonymous."

I stiffen, a bolt of curiosity and intrigue shooting through me. I once asked Aaron to do the same, and him not wanting to was one of many things that led to our downfall. But, fuck, I dream about it: the fear of trying to escape from someone while hoping they'll catch me, their sole intention to take me roughly.

"Sounds far-fetched," I manage.

Gwen shrugs. "I said it more as a joke, 'cause no one knows if he's real or not. I've only heard of it happening once since coming to town, and who knows if she was bullshitting for drama or not." She glances down at her phone. "Oh, I should get going. Text you later." With a final wave, she's out the door, and I return to cleaning the front, getting it ready for the supper shift when Fawn takes over.

Time ticks away, five o'clock steadily approaching. Normally, this is around the time I get eager to be finished, but now I'm wondering what's expected when Jace shows up.

If he comes.

Being with Aaron taught me how flighty men can be. How forgetful they are when they don't really want something; surely Jace was only friendly because of the past.

When the door chimes, I glance up from mopping the entire floor, but instead of a customer, it's my boss.

"Hi, you're early." She normally arrives around four-thirty, but it's only four.

Fawn grabs the mop from me, already angling the bucket of dirty water to wheel to the back room, despite my resistance. "I would have been in sooner if I didn't have an appointment. Jim called earlier and mentioned what happened this morning, you poor thing. That boy isn't welcome here anymore." She glances at the coffee stains near my ankles, a dried crustiness I've had to get used to. "I'm sorry you dealt with that. You can head home early."

The tiredness from the day battles with my depressingly empty bank account, leaving me with no response other than nervously shifting my feet. Reality is a shitty thing, weighing on my chest. The constant emails reminding me of late payments are a reminder I seriously can't afford to leave early. Hell, I should be begging her to work longer shifts.

"I, uh...can't." *Because I can't afford to.* "I mean, I don't mind working 'til five. It's only an hour more, and—"

"You'll be paid for the entirety of your shift, Payton," she says in a deliberate, knowing tone. "Consider it an apology for my customers harassing you."

My heart thumps faster, her kindness too generous for comfort. "Oh, you don't need to. It's okay."

"It *is* okay," she agrees. "It's okay for you to go home early, have a break, and unwind from this morning without worrying yourself about a smaller paycheque." She pats my hand as she passes, clearly finished discussing this. "Go home, Payton. Thanks for all your hard work."

"Alright." Who am I to argue?

I follow her to the back to retrieve my purse and hang up my apron. After a wave to both owners, I head for the front, noting it's an hour earlier than when I agreed to meet with Jace.

I stare down the road like he'll miraculously appear. Gwen's voice slips into the crevices of my mind, rebuking me for not waiting, for not doing more to reconnect with him.

Old friends or not, who the hell would want to talk to me, mess and all? Besides, it begins with a conversation, then the egg hunt. Then he'll ask for a date, the date will lead to a relationship, and then he'll become a villain like Aaron is and—

Holy fuck, slow down.

My heart beats so rapidly, it'll burst through my chest if I'm not careful. My mind got away from me, anxiety driving it to extreme heights where I'm imagining every worst outcome.

Amidst my mini anxiety attack, I miss the person who appears in front of me until his sneer is impossible to ignore. His eyes are more manic than earlier, when he was feigning a guise in front of his friends.

Without speaking a word, I whirl on my heel to get away. He's quick in grabbing my elbow, though, his fingers pinching me tight enough to gain my submission. For now, at least. After a hopeful scan of the area, I realize, depressingly, no one's around to overhear or help.

"What the fuck do you want, Aaron?"

"You went to my uncle yesterday morning. Bad form. Keep acting like this, and I'll have to remind you what little power you have."

I jerk my arm away, bringing my purse between us as a form of defence. "After three creepy notes, I'm sick of whatever game this is."

"Again with the notes." His lips pull to the side in a smirk, but knowledge from a relationship with him proves he's masking a lie, even though we're alone.

"I know your handwriting. Leave me alone, Aaron." I despise how my tone slips into old apprehensions. "What's the purpose, anyway? You cheated on me, bankrupted me. Why the *hell* would you want to get back together?"

He sways closer, his unfocused gaze latching onto the ground. It's then I smell what I missed before: the spicy whiff of alcohol burning my nose. He's drunk. "Because you've always been mine, Payton. I was all your firsts, and I'll sure as hell be your lasts too. You even *think* of letting another man touch what's mine, I'll gut him. And then you for being a whore."

Fear has my blood racing, but I find enough strength to push him away, knowing very well I could be initiating a fight I won't win—*especially* after his pitiful threats went full force into a real threat. "You're drunk. Go home and sleep it off, and I'll pretend none of this happened." Fat chance, but I'll give anything to end this conversation.

He sneers, his hand quick when he snatches my arm and drags me closer, our bodies touching for the first time in a year. I gag, both from the smell of alcohol and everything else to do with this cheating asshole.

"Only because you asked so nicely. I'll see you tonight. Sweet dreams."

Tonight?

My heart hammers as I watch him turn and walk away, disappearing around the corner. Tonight... What the fuck will tonight bring?

Out of seemingly nowhere, a black truck pulls up to the curb, its idling rumbles tuning every other noise out, even that of my racing mind. The passenger window rolls down, and I know whose face will appear even before he leans across the console.

"Fancy meeting you here, Thorne. Get in. I'll drive you home."

PAYTON STARES, her eyes blown wide like no one's offered her a drive home before.

Hell, I think *I* did once in the past, but she found a different way home from the party that night, opting to go with another classmate. I'll admit, that shit hurt, but she acted normal the next day at school, so I moved on and read nothing into it.

"Get in," I repeat, leaning over to the passenger door to pull the handle and push it open. It swings, nearly hitting her, but still, she stares down the road, debating if she's going to run or accept my offer.

After another moment, she sighs and climbs inside the truck, buckling up. Her eyes sweep the area, and that's when I notice her skin's a bit paler than earlier—a reaction I doubt having to do with my early arrival.

"You okay?"

"What?" She jerks my way, her throat swallowing. "Y-yeah. Good timing on your part, that's all."

She's hiding something, but I pull away from the curb and drive in the direction of her house, figuring the vehicle might not be the best place to get into it.

"I should consider myself lucky I was coming by early."

"Fawn heard what happened this morning and suggested I go home to relax." As I turn the corner away from the diner, she sends a final peek out the window before shrinking into the seat. Whatever happened, at least she's settling.

"That's nice of her." It's the least they can fucking do after the shit Bennett pulled. More than once, I debated hunting that fucker down to get a few more punches in today.

"Helping was nice of *you*."

"Nah." My fingers flex over the steering wheel as I turn down the single road near the edge of town, slowing down to prolong the trip. "It was the right thing to do. But I'm not here to debate ethics and morals, just see you."

I allow my eyes to leave the dirt road to study her, noticing the way she's pressed against the door to create as much space between us as she can. It's cute how skittish she's become, but also not, because it makes me want to destroy Bennett.

"Seeing you this morning wasn't expected." It was, because Brad mentioned her working there, but I won't admit that.

"Being back wasn't what I expected." It's a statement that opens the opportunity for me to ask for details, but her house comes into view, and I'll be damned if I'm beginning this kind of conversation for her to end it early. Plus, I still have to figure out what had her so spooked outside the diner.

I park in front of her house, and she twists to face me. "Thanks for the drive."

"No problem. It's kind of a far walk from here to the diner, especially when mornings still retain the frost. No car?"

"Can't afford one." Her cheeks flush red, and her lips roll together like she's said more than she meant to.

"I only afford this because it's a business write-off." Not completely true, but it quells the look on her face enough that the knot in my stomach begins unwinding.

Hand on the door, she pauses, her hair flicking over her shoulder as she twists back. "I'm not doing anything but relaxing, so if you're not busy...drink? I don't have beer, but I think I have wine. And pop. Water too."

Feeling like a damn victor, I turn the vehicle off and snag the keys and my wallet, then immediately hop out and around the front of the truck to finish opening her door, offering my hand to help her out.

Her hand, warm and fucking soft, slips into mine. "Gentleman."

"My mother raised me right. Are you telling me Bennett didn't help you from vehicles?" Teasing slips into my tone since we both know the answer to that, but it doesn't stop the shadow from passing over her expression—or the guilt I feel for bringing it up.

"Aaron didn't help me with much."

She leads me to her house, unlocking the door while I study the surrounding area, noting the place I hid when watching her through her window. The woods are vast, though I've never really had a reason to be this far away from home; nothing's over here except a forest that eventually connects with the next town's boundaries.

"Coming?" She glances over her shoulder, holding the door open, and I stride up the two wooden steps with chipped blue paint and through the entrance.

It smells like her. Like morning dew right before sunrise, left behind by the night's chill. The chill I anticipate seeing her in very soon. There's a faint whiff of apple cider in the air as well, reminding me of the body spray she wore in high school.

At least not everything has changed.

She kicks off her shoes with a happy moan that does things to my dick, then rolls her neck before dropping her purse a few steps from the entrance. "Didn't realize how long of a day it's been. Feels good to be home."

She heads for the kitchen, leaving me standing in the small entrance cut out of the house—a three-by-three-feet tiled area consumed mainly by a shoe rack and coat closet. I kick off my shoes and step into the attached living room, noting the old-fashioned rug and couch.

"Take a seat," she calls from the kitchen. "Wine?"

I despise wine. "Sure."

She returns holding two glasses of red, handing me one before dropping onto one end of the couch. She sips her drink, some of the colour returning to her unusual paleness as I settle on the opposite end, stretching my legs out as far as the distance between me and the wooden coffee table allows for.

After a moment of awkward but comfortable silence, she releases a giggle and drops her head onto the couch's backing, eyes staring at the ceiling.

"What's funny?"

"This. You. Me. A year ago, I never imagined this being my future."

You and me both. "Didn't ever think you'd return to these parts, if I'm honest. You never even came to visit your parents on holidays."

"Moving back home wasn't part of the plan," she murmurs with a sigh before taking a long drink. I'm about to come out and ask what I'm dying to know when she rolls her head to the side, and her mouth spreads into a slow smile. "We never hung out in school, did we? Like outside of it, I mean."

"You hated me."

"And you hated me." Her smile expands, breaking open my chest bit by bit. "We both know we were lying on those fronts. Maybe we should have given actual friendship a shot."

"I'm happy we didn't," I reply with a tip of my glass, my words surprising even me. "What we had was perfect in our own way. Fun."

"You *tormented* me." She snorts. "Of course, it was fun for you!"

"Torment is such a strong word," I drawl in an almost mocking tone. "Let's not make it sound worse than it was."

Her laughter wakes a part of me that apparently went to sleep with her absence. A part that grins back. Like I told Brad, it's not like I sat around waiting for the woman. I dated others in the years past, but with her in front of me again, it's like none of them existed.

"You really are the same, Jace."

"So are you." Her face falls, laugh lines smoothing out for a frown of misery, and I'm kicking myself for making the happiness on her face disappear so quickly.

"I'm not the same. Not at all." Her voice gets thick with impending tears, but she forces them away behind a swig of wine.

This is my opening, and, this time, I won't miss.

"I have to ask…"

"I know." She sighs, her shoulders dipping like they're holding the weight of her world. Which, perhaps they are. "I don't know where to begin."

"You went to Guelph for school." She was excited to have gotten accepted to her dream school and journey across the country. I can recall her excitement like it was yesterday, the sight of her joy so damn beautiful. "For a vet med degree."

"Yeah." She sips her drink, sloshing the liquid around in her mouth as she considers. "I got the degree. Never made it to the job part, though. A few months after leaving here, Aaron texted me, saying he was in Kitchener, which is close to Guelph. We hung out a few times, and he used all the right words to get me back. A few months later, we got an apartment together halfway between the two cities. He drove to his school, while I took transit to mine since student loans and day-to-day expenses maxed me out, leaving no budget for even a cheap car. We graduated and moved to Toronto, figuring we'd both find work there. He wanted to live deep in the city, but I argued for the outskirts—like Ajax, Pickering, or Mississauga—to save money. It wasn't our first fight, which probably should have been a clue." She pauses before adding, "Clue number one million technically. God, I'm fucking stupid for making excuse after excuse for him."

"You're not stupid. You wanted it to work, so you rationalized his behaviours to yourself."

"No, I'm an idiot," she counters. "I continued to look the other way. He started saying how I'd changed over the years, and not for the better. I began stress eating, and he became uninterested. We were wildly incompatible in the bedroom. He was boring, and I wanted... more." She stops abruptly with a nervous chuckle, shaking her near-empty wine glass. "Fuck, what's in this stuff? Sorry for babbling."

"Babble all you want." *You're confirming what I hoped for.*

Red tinges her cheeks, but she shakes her head and continues. "It was one thing after another. And then the email came, saying my credit card had a huge balance owing. I assumed my card got hacked, until checking my account and noticing the kinds of purchases being made. So I confronted him, and learned despite him being well-off due to his parents, he maxed out my card and left me with the debt. Bars, clubs, restaurants...jewellery stores."

"He claims you cheated on him."

"Other way around."

The stem of the wine glass becomes fragile beneath my grip, and I wish I'd hit him harder this morning. Hard enough to send him six feet under, perhaps. While fire ignites within my veins, Payton keeps talking, her words only sparking the flames hotter.

"That was nearly a year ago, and given the hellish time we were together, I don't miss him. But he left me with a debt so high, I can't pay it all off. Add that to living expenses and paying back my student loans, life in Ontario got too unaffordable. I spoke with my parents, but they had nothing to help, except this place. They suggested I move back to save money by living here, then get a job to begin working at the debt. At the rate I'm going, I'll be living here the rest of my life."

I wouldn't mind that one bit, but the sentiment that she *must* will always linger.

"Sadly, there's no vet clinic in town for me to get a job at. Closest one is the next town over, but I couldn't walk it. Fawn was nice enough to give me a job. It's not even living here that's the problem either; in some ways, I'm okay with it. Being in big cities made me remember how much I enjoy small-town life, but when I learned Aaron, for some reason, returned too, that was a hard fucking pill to swallow. I swear, he knew I'd come running home, so he did too."

This whole conversation is a hard fucking pill to swallow.

"Anyway..." She stands, swinging her empty glass back and forth. "I think I need more. I'll be back."

And I think Bennett needs a fucking hammer to his skull.

EIGHT

PAYTON

STUPID, *stupid, stupid.*

Filling my wine glass to the brim probably isn't the best choice considering I'm blaming it for making me say as much as I have. Even though the little alcohol I've consumed technically can't be at fault, for the sake of going back to the living room, it is.

Jace Hayes isn't the person I thought I'd ever spill so much of my guts out to, and now he probably thinks I'm a freak. It feels nice to be *heard*, though. Gwen's been supportive, but she didn't attend school with us, so it's not the same. Jace knew me pre-breakup. He witnessed the beginning of Aaron and me, was forced to endure Aaron's antics when he'd come around our lockers, so it's almost fitting he hears about our ending too.

There's no reason I shouldn't tell him about the notes, or even Aaron's threats before he showed up. Unlike the police, who brushed me aside, Jace doesn't seem like he'd do that. Then again, I've already unloaded so much on him. It's been eight years, and if I reveal this, it might make him feel obligated to help. One of the promises I made myself after breaking up with Aaron was to never be reliant on a man again.

Taking my glass and my decision, I return to the living room and catch Jace's staring contest with my coffee table—ironically at the drawer hiding Aaron's notes. He loses the competition when I enter.

"You probably didn't want to hear all that." The couch sucks me back into my spot.

"I asked." His thick voice has an edge to it. "Bennett's a moron for fucking up the best thing that'll ever happen to him."

"I'm hardly a—"

"The best thing," he interrupts, his tone making my toes curl.

I can't recall the last time someone referred to me as the "best." Aaron never did, that's for sure.

Jace is still watching me attempt to make any sense of what's happening in my mind. Before I go insane trying, I say, "Your turn. Catch me up on what you've been doing."

Jace sips his drink before settling against the couch's arm. "I moved a few months after you did to get my apprenticeship in construction. Dad wanted me to take over the business, but I wanted to get all my certifications away from here, just to say I didn't spend my *whole* life in this small town. Dad got sick, so I returned sooner than intended. He stepped down, and a year after that, died."

"I'm sorry." I never met his father, but saw him around at schoolwide ceremonies. At one point, I think my parents hired him to fix the roof on our old house, but I would have been pretty young then.

He shrugs, taking another sip of his drink. "Part of life. Can't help dying."

That's one way to look at it.

"You happy?"

"With the business? Absolutely. Work is steady. Jobs come in often. We get a lot of municipal and provincial contracts. Currently, we're building a new neighbourhood in the next town over."

"That's really cool. It'd be nice to own a business. I'd love to open my own vet clinic one day." Dreams require money, though, and I don't have any, so they're long on hold.

"You'd make a kick-ass vet, Payton. I'd bring my dog to you."

"You have a dog?"

"No." He smirks. "But if I did, I'd bring him to you."

"Him?"

"I always imagined myself with a male bulldog. Something about their faces gets me every time."

High school me would be rolling to know I'm discussing dog breeds with Jace Hayes.

"What about you? Dog or cat?"

"Why not both?" My gaze follows him as he rests his now-empty glass on the table. "More?"

"Nah, I should get going soon." He glances toward the door, and my stomach can't help but feel ripped apart. What began as an uncertain reunion shifted to something I've grown attached to. Clearly, loneliness is a thing, even if I've believed I haven't been.

"Sure." I stand to take his glass to the kitchen, but as my fingers graze the stem, he manacles his hand around my wrist, pulling me to a standstill between his legs. He tips his head back to see my face.

"He's an idiot, Payton. Anyone else he was with during your relationship is a pale imitation of you."

As though my heart wasn't already about to hammer out of my chest, because this is *Jace Hayes* of all people, he releases my wrist to instead grab my waist, repositioning me closer until my knees hit the couch. My arms are awkward by my sides, the urge to rest them on his wide shoulders growing strong, but also uncertain.

High school me would have showered in chlorine before allowing Jace to touch me in any way that didn't involve yanking on my hair or rifling through my stuff to steal my only pen—typical shit he pulled. Very glad I've grown up from being that girl.

"You're gorgeous," he murmurs, his grip tightening. "You miss him?"

"No. A few weeks after the breakup, I realized I was more pissed off than sad. Hurt, but not for the reasons you think." *Maybe this is the time. Tell him about the notes. Just do it!*

"I wish I hit him a bit harder this morning."

"I do too." Normally, I'm not a violent person, but the satisfactory image of Aaron being taken away on a stretcher is an appealing temptation—*especially* after what he said earlier.

"Next time," he promises, one hand releasing my hip to skate over the front of my stomach—over what, for a long time, was the most vulnerable part of me. Sometimes, it still is when I allow it to be.

"You're smiling."

Was I? "Thinking of the past."

"What about?

"That past me would have died before letting you touch me."

"Funny," he murmurs in a dry, unamused tone countering his comment, "because past me would have died *to* touch you."

My breath catches, the impact of what he's saying barreling into me. That means—

If that's the case, every secret fantasy he starred in could have come true. Things would have been different, and I never would have taken Aaron back, meaning the past eight years could have gone so vastly different; I wouldn't be swimming in debt, or receiving stalkerish threats from my ex.

Jace and Aaron are so opposite; it's amazing they didn't kill each other during school with their animosity or blow up the building or something. Which means whenever Jace glared at Aaron hanging around my locker, was he jealous?

A hand cuts into my vision. "Lost you."

He can't know where I went.

As he slides away, the jagged white line on the back of his hand catches my attention again. I noticed it this morning when he was drinking coffee and was immediately curious about its origins.

I stop his hand from lowering, thumb brushing the scar. "What's the story here?"

"Work. Drill slipped, sliced my hand. It could have been much worse if not for reflexes."

"Dangerous life you lead," I joke softly.

"Only if you're not paying attention."

There's nothing else to say, but I remain between his legs—a place I should back away from, to remember what the purpose of me being in town *isn't*. Perhaps Gwen is right. Not necessarily about sex, but about Jace, trying a friendship with him not built around teenage antics.

"Are you going to the Easter hunt?"

A smirk plays along his lips, and he readjusts his hat, a nervous twitch I've seen him do many times in the past. "I debated it. You?"

"Same."

"Maybe I'll see you there."

"Maybe."

Oh, look at me go. Woman of many words. In my defence, I didn't really try with Aaron, so I don't know how to do this...whatever *this* is. Maybe that says something about us, though.

Left with nothing else, I blurt the first thing that randomly comes to mind: the second half of my conversation with Gwen. "Heard a rumour about some guy sometimes coming around at Easter to host his own egg hunt. A private one, where he hunts a woman. Have you heard of him?"

Jace tips his head farther back, his dark eyes somehow becoming a shade closer to midnight. "I've heard of him, yeah. Haven't seen him, if that's what you're asking. Though if the rumours are correct, I'm not his type."

"Hm."

Jace's hands slide a few inches down my thighs as he leans back, regarding me curiously. "It scare you? Someone being out there like that?"

No, what scares me is my ex-boyfriend threatening anyone I may sleep with in the future. How much more do I admit, considering what I said earlier? How much more embarrassment can I handle?

"No."

Huh. Guess a lot more.

Since I've said that much, I continue down the path of self-destruction. "That was something that drove Aaron and me apart. I wanted more...like that. Fantasies he refused to entertain. Sex with him was boring—and maybe that's on me. But it should *feel* like more too, you know?" *No, he doesn't know. Shut up and stop embarrassing yourself.* "I mean, there's more I'd be interested in trying."

"You two weren't meant for one another. There's nothing wrong with that." He pulls his hat off again, runs a hand through his curls, then replaces it on his head. "Would you? Do that, I mean? Willingly get chased through the woods by a masked man, knowing you'd be fucked at the end."

If I knew I wasn't going to be murdered, sure.

My skin ignites like it's on fire, basically telling him my answer before opening my mouth. "I like the concept of it and the heart-pounding fear it'd bring. The adrenaline. I'd try it, yeah."

Jace nods once, his hands sliding farther down my jeans as he falls back against the couch. It's in his slight movement I feel him slipping away, like I've fucked up.

He glances at the door, and it's enough of a hint I turn for his wine glass to take it back to the kitchen, not wanting him to see my face while composing myself. What changed? What did I allow myself to feel for those thirty seconds?

Perhaps he thinks like Aaron; my interests aren't normal.

Either way, I know a brush-off when I feel one, so I swallow the ache and stride back to the living room, finding him lingering by the door with his shoes already on. His hands are stuffed in his pockets, and he seems as awkward as I feel.

"I'll see you around. Maybe tomorrow, at the diner."

"Great."

Hand on the knob, he glances over his shoulder. "Sorry Bennett fucked everything up, but I'm not sorry you're back."

And with that confusing and contradictory statement, he leaves. A moment later, the rumble from his truck fills the room, and I watch out the window as he disappears down the road.

SLEEP EVADES me because I'm ramrod still lying in bed, waiting for the moment Aaron shows up. Beside me, my phone rests unlocked, 9-1-1 already typed on the screen. The moment I hear him, they'll be receiving a call, and then his police chief uncle can look me in the face tomorrow when I say, *Told you.*

Around 3 a.m., sleep sweeps me away, and outside remains silent.

Aaron never comes.

Asshole was only trying to trick me.

NINE

JACE

THE HURT on her face nearly broke me. I hadn't meant to leave so abruptly, but after her confirmation, leaving was the only way to not reveal all my secrets. The only reason I didn't act before we're both ready.

Once night falls and I feel she's tucked into bed, I leave a note on her porch for her to find in the morning.

I'M FEELING HUNGRY, LITTLE RABBIT. UP TO OUR OWN PERSONAL EGG HUNT?
BE ON THE LOOKOUT SATURDAY FOR FURTHER INSTRUCTIONS.

If only I could witness her finding it, but coming by in the morning might mean being unable to walk away.

On my way back to my truck parked way down the road, movement in the bushes catches my attention. The cool night air makes my breath visible as white clouds and I pause, scanning the area again for what's most likely a bird or small animal.

Still...my nerves tense, and I find myself striding in the direction I heard the noise from, hands sliding out from my pockets in case it's something more dangerous than a small creature.

At the bush, there's nothing obvious, and I scan the surrounding area before glancing back to Payton's house, not enjoying the sensation of something being *wrong*. Having had enough, I decide I can't leave her and double back, remaining in the treeline close to the house to keep an eye on things...just in case.

It's hours later when I accept it must have been a squirrel or other small animal and head home, knowing work tomorrow will fucking suck after a short night's rest.

BRAD BOUNDS behind me as I head for my truck after dismissing the guys for an hour-long lunch break. On the passenger seat, I grab the rag, wiping sweat, dirt, and hopefully exhaustion from my brow before replacing my hat and heading for the driver's side. As I thought last night, by the time I returned home, showered, ate, and settled, sleep was too short to handle today.

By the time I'm behind the wheel, Brad's slipping into the passenger seat. "I assume you're going for lunch at Fawn's, and it's been forever since I had a grilled cheese from that place. Figured I'd tag along and watch you make an ass out of yourself over the pretty waitress."

"Shut your mouth." I shove his arm, his joke stoking my jealousy. He has no right thinking of Payton like that.

"Testy."

Thankfully, his focus switches, mainly commenting on his wife's hourly bathroom breaks all night and complaining about our lumber delivery, which was supposed to arrive this morning but is now delayed until after the holidays.

The complaints carry us inside the diner, where I immediately seek out Payton. She's serving a family across the room, her movements jerky and hair frazzled as she heads to another table to fill mugs. There's some twenty tables in the diner, and over half of them are filled, the restaurant a buzz of conversation in every volume possible.

"Busy," Brad comments, leading us toward two free stools at the counter.

Payton spots us while cleaning a table before carrying a mountain of plates and cups to the back room. She returns after a moment, her breath a series of short puffs as she scrambles for her pad and pen in her apron's pocket.

"Hey, sorry, what can I get you?" She glances back and forth, waiting for one of us to speak. I let Brad go first, studying her for any sign she's hurt about last night.

"Grilled cheese and coffee for me, please."

"Same," I say, "and a glass of water."

"Got it." She jots it all down and quickly rushes to the back, presumably to put our order in with Jim. She's back quickly, carrying a tray of food to another table.

"Jesus, you have it bad."

"Fuck off." There's more I want to say, but Payton slips behind the counter again, reaching for two mugs and a glass to fill our drink orders.

"Sorry for the delay," she murmurs, eyes low. She hasn't looked at me yet, giving me the sense she is still bothered by yesterday—making me feel even shittier. She has no fucking idea how tempted I was to take our reunion, then skip over friendship and straight into having her ride me on that blue couch of hers.

I bring my mug close, and Brad takes his, but I nudge the water her way. "Drink," I demand. "You're run off your feet."

She takes the cup with a smile before placing it onto her side of the counter and rushing to the back at a chime.

On and on it goes while Brad and I sip our coffees. He talks about the upcoming holiday while I visually stalk Payton. We were the last customers to enter for the lunch rush, so the last to get our food, which is perfectly fine since it means she'll finally be free to stay in one place.

"I'm sorry." She sets two plates in front of us before glancing at the clock. "You probably don't have a lot of time to eat."

"Good thing he's boss," Brad mutters with a nudge to my ribs. "Gets to decide when we start working and all that."

While it may be true, the rest of the guys will return at one, so it'd look bad if we don't. Besides, I'd rather do what we can today, considering the upcoming holidays and delivery delays.

"This place is packed, and we're fast eaters. No worries."

With a grateful nod, she goes and cleans up a few of the now-abandoned tables as people slowly finish their meal and leave. Brad and I finish eating, and Payton returns to ring up our bill. Before she finishes at the register, I slide her a fifty-dollar bill.

"I'll get you change."

"Don't. It's yours."

Brad snorts while pretending to be suddenly interested in the cheap decorations, most notably, a plastic bunny nearby.

"Your total is just over twenty. You can't give me a thirty-dollar tip." She continues staring at the money like it'll bite her.

"It's already done. Get the change, Payton."

Shockingly, she obeys, returning with two bills.

Her teeth scrape over her bottom lip, her inner battle wavering as she murmurs, "I don't want your handouts just 'cause you know the truth."

I take the cash before reaching for her, slipping a finger between the apron's tie and using it to drag her close enough to slip the bills into her front pocket, lingering for a few seconds because I can't help myself.

"They're not a handout. They're for being a kick-ass waitress."

Her cheeks flush. "It's not that difficult to bring people food."

"It is dealing with the assholes people can sometimes be. Need I remind you about yesterday?"

"Fine," she mutters with an eye roll that does things to me. It's cute she thinks she had a choice.

A brief check of my phone tells me time is up, so I lift to my feet, Brad following me up. He takes my stare as a hint and shoots Payton a two-fingered salute. "See you around."

"Bye," she replies as he walks away, her attention lingering on me.

Once the door chimes shut behind him, I finally have her all alone. I want to ask about the note, but that'd defeat the purpose in anonymity. I also want to reassure her she didn't scare me off last night—not in the way she assumes, anyway. I ran because I was scared to touch her before we're both ready, and if I touched her, I wouldn't stop.

But I don't say any of that. Instead, my hands go for her apron again to pull her flush against the counter while leaning as close as I can. My fingers linger by her cheek, tracing skin so fucking soft, I can already imagine what she'll look like beneath the moon. I tuck a few stray strands of hair around her ear before tracing down her jawline, pausing by her mouth.

"I'll be seeing you soon, Payton."

Outside, I nearly collide with someone passing the diner, and it's his face that makes me wish I pushed the door open with more impact. Aaron Bennett sneers.

"She wasn't yours then, and she isn't now. She always comes back to me, so stop sniffing around."

My fingers link into his shirt, and I yank him closer, aware of the slowing cars driving by anticipating a fight they'll no doubt report to his uncle, the chief of police. Since we're in public, I limit myself to a single statement, because I'll be damned if the asshole gets me arrested for assault before tomorrow. The tiny police force will get such a hard-on for *finally* receiving actual work, I won't see the outdoors for at least a day—and I'd miss my own hunt.

"Stay the fuck away from her. I'll do more for her than you ever could. For one, I'll fuck her in ways she'll actually enjoy."

Red creeps up his neck, and he pushes away, his fist swinging but easily impeded. "Fuck you. You know nothing about us. She's a goddamn whore who can't—"

I don't let him finish, hauling him closer, so he can see how fucking serious I am when it comes to her. A quick glance shows no one but Brad is paying attention, his amused face practically pushed against the passenger window of my truck.

"You say one more damn thing against her, and she'll be gifted your teeth as a necklace. Do *not* test me."

"You're all talk, Hayes. You won't do shit. I can have your business shut down like that." He snaps his fingers, the reminder of what his daddy's money, as town mayor, could be capable of with just cause.

"You touch my business or Payton, and it'll be the last thing you do."

Before I act on those dreams and ruin ones that'll hopefully come true tomorrow, I release him and head for my truck.

TEN

PAYTON

IT'S SO NOT REAL, *just fictional stories to entertain the women of this town, same as how parents sell the concept of a giant, fuzzy animal hopping between houses delivering chocolate, other sweets, and little toys to children.*

This is what I tell myself all day as I pace the house Saturday, the note gripped in my hand. Normally, I wouldn't consider myself a superstitious person, but after speaking with Gwen and Jace, this rumoured guy might be possible.

Last night, when listening for Aaron's footsteps, *someone* showed up. When I saw the paper this morning, I immediately assumed my ex, but once unfolding it, the jagged words written with urgency weren't in Aaron's handwriting.

I'M FEELING HUNGRY, LITTLE RABBIT. UP TO OUR OWN PERSONAL EGG HUNT?
BE ON THE LOOKOUT SATURDAY FOR FURTHER INSTRUCTIONS.

This *has* to be a joke. Gwen said it hasn't happened in years—*if* the last report was true. It's too much of a coincidence it happens to me so soon after learning about it.

Unless Gwen's in on it. Even as the thought passes through my head, I know my anxiety is ruling my logic.

This can't be real. It's having me pacing my house half the day, worrying over *nothing.* Whoever wrote this note is fucking with me. While it's not Aaron's handwriting, it could be one of his friends'. That'd be the cherry on top of Aaron's torment.

Or worse: Jace. After his strange behaviour the other night, is this his ultimate prank? Although, he seemed fairly normal yesterday when he and Brad dropped by for lunch, even giving me a large tip.

Or a severe case of gaslighting is happening.

Crack.

I freeze, gaze darting to the front door.

No. Fucking. Way.

It's an animal, nothing more. A squirrel.

A squirrel wouldn't make the entire porch crack, logic reminds me.

At this point, I'll take Aaron looming to scare me.

In case it is, I rush toward the kitchen, grabbing the largest knife from the knife block. A fighter I am not, but any form of defence is better than nothing, because *if* someone's there, and that someone is wearing a mask, I'm still not convinced this guy isn't a serial killer who plants rumours to lure people in with the promise of sex.

Weapon in hand, I run for the front door, almost laughing at myself. Running toward a potential killer screams all sorts of saneness, yet I don't pause as I yank the door open, freezing at the sight.

"Fuck."

I can't be certain who said that—him or me. Maybe both.

Gwen was right, or someone's playing a *really* cruel trick.

Because there he is. A fucking massive shadow himself, a man wrapped in all black—pants, tee, sweater, and a wolf mask covering half his face—backing up from a golden egg about the size of a football.

"Who the fuck are you?" I lift the knife, gripping it harder to hide the quivers radiating down my arms. If I have any chance of convincing this guy I'm capable of defending myself, not shaking is probably the first step.

Instead of running away, Wolf Man steps onto the porch, only the egg separating us. He wasn't supposed to approach the weapon. Maybe he's crazier than I am. I press into the door at my back, mentally calculating how long it'll take to slip inside and lock the door.

"Do you even know how to use that thing?" His voice is deep, throaty, and almost familiar. I've definitely heard it in passing; someone around town perhaps. Probably someone I've served at the diner.

One of Aaron's friends playing a cruel trick?

"Slice and cut. How hard does it have to be?"

Beneath the edge of the mask, his mouth curves upward in a mocking grin. It irritates me to no end that he doesn't believe I'd be able to save myself.

"You're different than the others. It's refreshing."

Other*s*. Plural. Gwen missed a few facts.

"Different because I have self-respect and don't want a masked serial killer to off me?"

Dark eyes clash with mine—also strangely familiar. They hold mine captive, a jail I have no desire to break out of. "If I were a serial killer, you'd be dead already."

"Maybe you're waiting until a better time?"

In a flash, he moves. Suddenly, I'm backed inside my house, the door left open. Instinct drives the knife up with no particular aim. His large hand, covered in a black, leather glove catches my wrist and pins it to the wall above my head. By the time my brain works well enough to recall having two arms, he's capturing the other one, also lifting it above my head.

"Now..." He ducks his head, his breath warm on my face. "You were saying?"

"Let me go." My swallow is rough; my breath staggered. Fear tenses every nerve, but there's something oddly thrilling about this too. As long as he isn't going to kill me, that is. Something exhilarating and stimulating at the idea of this stranger.

"I will, because we have a game to play later."

"Take your egg and fuck off. Choose someone else. Not interested."

Lie.

I spent all day dreading this possibility, but now I've seen him and know he's real? Beneath the logic that's driven me through life this far—though look how shitty that's been working for me—there's something that speaks to his own craziness. Something darker. After Aaron, something deserving.

It's also everything *with* Aaron making me hesitate. Being hunted by a stranger in the same week my crazy ex is leaving notes doesn't seem smart.

His chest rumbles against mine with his chuckle, those sinful lips curling. The wolf mask covering most of his face emits danger. "You're very interested." His eyes dip down as his tongue flicks against his top lip.

I follow his gaze to—*oh, for fuck's sake, why didn't I put on a bra?* My nipples are hard, evidence of my lie.

"Door's open. It's cold."

He huffs his laughter, walking into me. My heart flutters in my chest, and my mouth parts with the start of a scream no one's around to overhear. It's quickly stolen by his fingers pressing so hard into my wrist, the knife slips from my grip and onto the ground between us. My scream transforms into a whimpered "ow."

The sudden proximity makes me realize how *big* he is. How, as he's pressed into me, I feel every hard plane. How the thin tank I'm wearing is basically nothing, and the sick part of my mind wants him to rip it off.

"If you weren't interested, you'd be putting up a much better fight—kicking, screaming, hitting. You'd be trying to get free, but you're not." He squeezes my wrists, emphasizing both his words and the truth I'm hiding from even myself. "Deep down, you're like me. You want this. You crave being hunted through the woods like an animal, to never know where I am at any given time. Wondering if your next step will be your last. How, *when* I catch you, I'll take you. How many orgasms you'll receive. And you'll be good, won't you? You won't go easy on me. This cute little show you've greeted me with is an appetizer for the meal. That's what I want. Fight me, little rabbit. Show me why the wolf should fear the prey."

I want all of that.

Fuck.

He grins with a quick flash of teeth before glancing at the knife by our feet. "And if that's your thing, I'll play along. Not like you'll ever nick me with it."

His breath trails along my neck as he slowly lowers his head, but not before his lips, surprisingly soft, caress my cheek. Before I realize what I'm doing, I turn my head slightly, following his path until his lips brush over mine. So light, it barely counts as a kiss, but it's a claim either way. A threat on its own.

An acceptance between us.

"How do I know you won't kill me?"

He grins before returning a bit of my power by releasing my hands. His finger traces my jaw, petting my pulse until it reacts. "Why would I kill who I desire the most?"

His eyes flash with excitement and the promise of more to come before abruptly spinning on his heel and exiting my house. Once again, I'm struck with the familiarity of that look. *Very* familiar...like recently stared into them familiar. A shade of brown so dark, in many ways they remind me of Jace's.

It takes me a moment to emerge from the maelstrom of my thoughts before chasing him onto the porch, but, like a ghost I've made up, he's gone, like he was never here.

But he was. The knife on the floor, the golden egg on the porch, and my insides in a tight knot are proof he was.

ELEVEN

JACE

AFTER PUSHING away from her and escaping out the door before I could say *fuck it all*, rip off the mask, and consume her right there, I disappear into the trees, heading to where my truck is parked in the far distance.

We're hours away from nighttime, and I won't spend the day stalking her from afar while being forced to ignore the anticipation.

No, it's all in her hands now.

My little rabbit will come to me in due time.

TWELVE

PAYTON

AN HOUR LATER, I've gotten the golden egg open and have read the note probably close to eight times over, pacing between *fuck no* and *maybe yes*.

It feels wrong, like I shouldn't want this.

Or because Aaron made you feel this is wrong?

But *fuck*, as messed up as it is, when he had me against the wall, that's what I've been chasing. The high, the thrill, the feeling of danger. What would a night in the woods feel like?

Freeing.

What would people think if this got out? Realistically, I shouldn't care, but I do.

Aaron would call me a whore, though nothing's really changing there.

Gwen would demand details.

And Jace...fuck. Nameless sex with a stranger who may be dangerous only days after reconnecting with him feels wrong. Almost like I'm cheating on him. Cheating on the prospect of what could be.

Could be? my inner voice chides. *He ran from you. He doesn't want you.*

It's not wrong, though. Even if Jace and I did spark a true friendship, what the man in the wolf mask offers may never come around again. I'd be giving up this chance for a will-he, won't-he situation with an old friend, who'll more than likely end up on the side of he won't.

All that's putting aside the way his eyes kind of remind me of Jace's. A fact that stalls my steps, gaze flicking back to the letter on my living room table. What if it's Jace? Gwen said no one's heard from this guy in years, yet it just so happens my first Easter back, *this* happens the day after admitting my desires to Jace.

What am I saying? Coincidence, nothing more.

I lift the letter, rereading it for what feels like the millionth time. Eventually, I'll be able to recite the damn thing.

LITTLE RABBIT,

THIS EASTER, I'D LIKE TO HOST MY OWN EGG HUNT WITH YOU.

THE INSTRUCTIONS ARE AS FOLLOWS:

IF YOU DO NOT CONSENT, PLACE THIS BACK ON YOUR PORCH, AND YOU WILL BE LEFT ALONE. I WILL REMOVE IT FROM YOUR HOME BY MIDNIGHT AND WILL NOT BOTHER YOU AGAIN. YOU WILL BE SAFE.

IF YOU CONSENT, KEEP THIS EGG INSIDE. AT EIGHT P.M., RUN FROM YOUR HOME. I WILL BE WATCHING, AND I WILL GIVE CHASE. YOU WILL NOT BE GIVEN ANY WARNING WHEN I'LL COME, BUT YOU WILL BE GIVEN A FEW MINUTES' HEAD START. DO NOT MAKE THE MISTAKE OF NOT USING THIS TIME TO GET AWAY.

IN THE WOODS, THERE ARE A FEW GOLDEN EGGS SCATTERED THROUGHOUT. SMALLER THAN THIS ONE—ABOUT THE SIZE OF YOUR PALM. EACH ONE WILL GRANT YOU A SINGLE

REQUEST YOU MAY CASH IN. FIND NONE, AND YOU'RE
COMPLETELY MINE TO USE HOW I PLEASE.

AS YOU HUNT, I'LL BE HUNTING YOU, SO BE SURE TO
HIDE WELL AND DON'T MAKE IT EASY. THE HARDER THE
CHALLENGE, THE BETTER THE THRILL FOR BOTH OF US.

WHEN I CATCH YOU, IF AT ANY TIME IT GETS TOO MUCH,
HERE ARE YOUR SAFE WORDS. MEMORIZE THESE. SAY THEM
ALOUD A FEW TIMES IF YOU MUST. I WILL NOT LEAVE
SCARRING DAMAGE. THAT IS NOT MY GAME.

SLOW DOWN: AMBER.

COMPLETE STOP: GOLDEN.

I'LL BE SEEING YOU LATER. HAPPY RUNNING, MY PREY.

No sign off, not that it's completely unexpected. He wouldn't want to give away his identity.

I stare at the ceramic, twist-top, golden-painted egg. I should place it back on my porch, arm myself for the night, and stay home. That's what I *should* be doing, because that's what someone sane would do.

But I'm not sane. And I don't think I have been for a long time. It'd be great to, for once, not listen to others' beliefs about how I should and shouldn't be and live for *me*. With Aaron, I turned everything off for the comfort of our relationship, but dating him was like wearing that one pair of shoes you can't get rid of, no matter how torn and ratty they are. There was a familiarity, though they never did the job, couldn't go fast enough. Still, even when I finally managed to toss them, they've reappeared, chasing me while *still* telling me how to live my life, this time by means of threats.

Beside the golden egg is the stack of credit card bills, all in my name, but not one cent of the debt is mine. I'm merely the neck the executioner slams the ax upon.

They're two sides of a coin: the egg and the bills. Paths laid, a direction needed.

The strict, no-nonsense side of me wants to place that egg back on the porch and deny today ever happened.

The side that needs a goddamn break from everything folds the note and places it inside the egg before twisting it shut, then carries it to my bedroom, where I hide it in the back of my closet—*not* putting it back outside, knowing by sundown I'll have signalled my intent.

It's one night.

A stranger.

A stranger who made my body come alive in the brief encounter.

I owe it to myself to do this.

And if he kills me...well, then I'll die a pleased person on one of the most sacred days of the year. That means something, doesn't it? If there's an afterlife, someone's bound to take pity on my horrible decision-making and pull me to the good side.

Back in the living room, I stare out the large window, not seeing my hunter. Except, he's there; I feel it deep down. He's watching the house —watching me. Waiting for my decision.

I settle onto the couch and wait for the hours to pass.

For him to realize I never placed the egg back outside.

THIRTEEN

JACE

SUN FALLS.

It's seven-thirty, and there's still no egg.

I knew she'd join me. Once she realized her own desires, it was a matter of convincing herself. Payton thinks through every little thing before making a decision, but she'll only choose what she feels is best.

There's still a half-hour, but agitation is the most unwelcome twist to my gut. Anticipation of what's to come. Old fantasies—though none were ever quite this level of depraved—will be played out tonight.

I remain in the shadows, phone gripped in my hand as the minutes go by, each one feeling endless.

Finally, we reach seven-fifty. Ten more minutes.

Nine...

Eight...

I push off the tree, approaching the house. I have every intention of following through on my deal and giving her the head start, but I want to be closer when she runs. Fear is half the thrill, but *Payton's* fear makes me groan thinking about it. When I face her tomorrow, will I be able to talk with her like a friend when I've been buried inside her pussy? When I know what she feels like when she comes. How she sounds. What she looks like.

My tongue sweeps along my bottom lip, my cock twitching in anticipation.

It's been a very long time since I've done this, and the last woman didn't fully understand what she signed up for, quickly learning this isn't something she's interested in. The night ended earlier than anticipated.

Payton, I already suspect, will be perfect. If I have one reservation, it's that she is unaware the man in the wolf mask is me.

At seven-fifty-seven, the door opens, and Payton steps out onto the porch, her gaze flitting to the trees fencing her home. She passes over me three times, but being too far away, too tucked into the shadows, she can't spot me.

But I see her. My prey. My little rabbit.

She's dressed in sensible clothing: yoga pants that merge with bright-pink sneakers—a point in my favour—a sweater zipped up half-way, and signs of a sports bra peeking from beneath.

It makes me smile, because it's proof she'll *try*.

Seven-fifty-eight. Two more minutes.

She steps off the porch.

Seven-fifty-nine. She scans the woods again before choosing a direction, taking off into the night, heading behind the house. The shadows quickly swallow her up, and then she's gone from sight.

The time on my phone changes to eight p.m.

Time to hunt.

Five minutes is my standard waiting time, but with Payton, I'm torn between breaking my own rules and following her sooner or giving her more time, letting her get as far away as she can.

The minutes tick away agonizingly slow. Finally, it's seven minutes past eight, and I slide my phone safely away in my chest pocket beside the switchblade.

I ensure the mask is tied tight enough.

Then, I hunt.

Run, little rabbit, run. I'm coming for you.

FOURTEEN

PAYTON

I THINK I've fucked up.

I think I'm majorly unprepared for what I've agreed to.

I think, even as I've only been running a matter of minutes, I'm about to hit a level of nirvana I long assumed was out of reach.

As my arms and legs pump, eyes scanning the darkness for even a smidge of a shadow moving, as fear—*true* fear—resonates through me, I've never been more thrilled, more excited, more turned on.

Hair whipping around, I try to see behind me, but the forest is too obscure to make out anything farther than a few tree lengths away. When he starts pursuing me, I'll have no hope of seeing him coming.

Him, or these eggs I'm supposed to find. Even as I dash forwards, I'm aware I should slow down and study the base of each tree, but there are so many. He can't possibly believe I'll succeed in this.

I take a sharp turn, changing direction. These woods are only so large, so hopefully he'll assume I stuck to running straight.

Essentially, the forest is a cage for me to hide in.

To hide and seek. My gaze passes over a few trees, seeking colourful fake eggs I have *no* idea when he would have hidden around. Eventually, I slow to a jog, hoping there's enough distance between us that a different pace won't change much.

If these eggs are even real. There's no telling he hid anything out here. There's not even proof he'll follow me.

What if this is some cruel trick, and I'm running for nothing?

But what if it's not?

I met my hunter. I spoke with him. He was real. He *felt* real, like this isn't a joke.

My steps slow to a walk and then a complete stop, hand against the nearest tree as my breaths release in large gasps. I'd die for a glass of water right about now. Turns out, I needed that head start, because apparently I'm *very* out of shape. At this rate, I'll be dead by the time he finds me.

Hope he enjoys fucking a corpse.

I walk on, changing directions again. It feels like I've been running for a while—if my lungs are any form of measurement—so who knows how far my house is. Surely he didn't hide anything out *this* far?

I stop, turn, and try to retrace my steps to determine which way my house is. Even then, I'm only seventy percent positive the route is correct. He won't assume I'll be running *toward* him, so he'll continue, giving me a chance to find the mysterious eggs likely hidden closer to my house.

If this plan doesn't work how it should, well, I still win in the end.

I *want* him to find me.

I want him to fuck me.

I want to be owned in all the ways I've once fantasized about.

The sticks crack beneath my retraced steps.

FIFTEEN
JACE

I FUCKING *LOVE* THE HUNT.

Sometimes I run, sometimes I walk, but I always listen. For the slight noises. The chirp of scurrying animals. The wind, because it's likely she'll run away from it, not into it.

When I pass two hidden eggs, clearly undiscovered, I presume she's gotten pretty far. The others are in the opposite direction, so if she keeps running this way, she's skipping them all.

I continue on, alternating between jogging and walking, switching my pace and direction every so often. The farther I go, the less noise there is. The wind dies entirely. Animals hole up for the night, undisturbed by civilization. Darkness blankets every inch, the moon above no bigger than a sliver, limiting the glow.

And then, amidst the silence, I hear it.

A crack.

I stop, eyes roving. Once, twice, until the faintest motion in the distance catches my attention. A spot of black breaking away from the rest, her hair streaming in a wave, and those damn pink sneakers giving her away. She runs nearby, not bothering to check her surroundings.

She's doubled back to trick me; if it wasn't for the noise, she might have gotten away with it too.

"Sneaky little rabbit," I murmur, following her on her new course. My steps pick up to a jog; fast enough she remains in view while also not catching up.

When I tire of this, I'll move on, make her *really* hide when she's aware I'm behind her and escape is the only option. This, right now, is a warm up. A game of hide and seek while she completes her egg hunt —which she's utterly failing at.

She is going in the right direction for one of them, so maybe she'll get lucky.

If she finds one, the deal is she makes her own request. And what Payton would demand is entirely a question for me, but one I anticipate getting taught the answer to.

"Yes!" she hisses from afar, her soft voice carrying over the wind. Presuming she found an egg, my mouth forms the closest thing I can to a smile. Seems I will be getting to learn her wishes after all.

It's almost upsetting how her cheer announced her exact location. Stepping behind a crowd of bushes and trees I know the egg was hidden at the base of, I watch as she tucks the ceramic blue egg in her sweater's pocket before taking off again without checking her surroundings.

Isn't that a shame.

She runs left, so I follow, jogging faster. Now, she's allowed to learn I'm nearby. I crave her fear, her tears, her little cries. I want her body to anticipate what's about to happen, to crave me the same as I do her. To the point she's needy, begging me to take her.

As I follow, I imagine everything I'll do to her, and in every position. On her hands and knees, getting scratched by the broken twigs and leaves. After we desecrate its peace, it'll take its boon from her skin. Against a tree, perhaps with a low-hanging branch I can tie her to. She'll be the perfect little prey, just waiting for me to eat her up.

My cock twitches in my pants just thinking about her taste. She'll be sweet, undoubtedly. She'll quench a thirst I've had entirely too long; a craving unsated for eight fucking years. She'll be bliss wrapped up in a pretty package, all fear and desire—a paramount combination.

She'll fight me like the feral little rabbit I know her to be, because this morning teased the possibility. Fuck, I *want* her to fight me, bite me, and hit me, being as animalistic as I plan on being to her.

She slows to a walk, probably assuming I'm far away. She's growing winded, going by her panting and rising shoulders.

I enter between two trees, pressing more weight into my steps until the ground announces my arrival. Payton freezes, her gaze jerking in my direction. Even in the dark, I spot the moment she stops breathing. When she realizes she's been caught. So I speak, just loud enough that nature carries my voice to her.

"Hunt's over, little rabbit, and you're caught in my snare."

SIXTEEN

PAYTON

CRACK.

That wasn't me...

Fuck.

He emerges from between two trees, his steps laid carefully, like a wolf seconds before it strikes; a tribute to his mask, no doubt. He's a source of sin, prowling toward his retribution—to me. His hood is drawn up, the same mask as earlier covering the top half of his face, and he approaches slowly, calculated, almost ghostly.

My feet are heavy, breaths coming out in rapid, exhausted pants. My body is too drained to keep going, yet I *want* to. Knowing it's only a matter of time until he catches me—again—and anticipating him doing so doesn't overshadow my desire to continue this.

The egg in my pocket feels heavy at his advance, and I'm tempted to reveal I've found one; there's a part of me that seeks his praise for a job well done within an impossibly dark forest.

"Found you," he announces, his voice low and gravelly, making my thighs clench. "Now what? Gonna be good for me? Lie down and take it the way you're meant to."

I may have considered it, if not for the challenge ringing in his tone, like he wants me to keep fighting.

So I do.

I turn and bolt, hearing the exact second he takes off after me.

A quick peek over my shoulder throws hair into my face, and it's with a rapid flurry I push the strands away to see him streaking after me. He's fast, easily eating up the distance between us. I push my legs a bit harder, forcing strength into muscles long worn out and used more tonight than since ever.

My arms pump for speed, my heart pounding like it's about to break free of my chest. Adrenaline is the only reason I'm still going, or else I'd be keeled over dead by now. How I'm going to have the energy to maintain what he's about to do to me, I have no fucking idea.

Regardless, I run, hearing his approach. *Feeling* how he's trailing me. Every sense is attuned to him. When I step, he takes two. For every three of my pants, he releases one measured exhale. Right down to my veins, my blood, it all centres on the man in the mask.

I chance another look and—

"Shit!" He's close. Only a couple strides away and—

Branches and leaves twist together, tangling around my ankle and causing me to become unbalanced. If I believed in the supernatural, I'd say nature is on his side.

Rolling onto my back while ignoring the stinging pain in my hands and knees, I wait until he's in sight, slowly approaching as though we're both uncertain what his next move will be. His pace suggests I won't run again, and his head ticks to the side, his smirk as wolfish as the mask covering the upper half of his face.

"Caught in a trap," he muses, kicking the ground by my feet. "Isn't that a shame?"

"Is it?" I find myself asking, unsure of what I'm supposed to do now; his golden egg left so few instructions. Not knowing what's about to happen sends a flood of heat between my legs.

"For you." White teeth flash in the darkness, the final thing I see before he reaches for me. I crab walk backwards, more of a messy scramble than anything. He makes a humming noise, then reaches again.

"Try harder," I taunt within a moment of brazenness before spinning around, one shoe jamming into the dirt and hoisting me upright. With a lunge, I take off running, wondering what's gotten into me.

This is *fun*.

He isn't holding back this time. His curse flies after me, his steps coming up fast before two arms capture my body, one around my waist and the other around my neck. He hauls me to a standstill, trapping me against his chest.

His chuckle is a warm, trickled taunt down the side of my neck. "You put up a good fight, but you've lost. You won't be getting away again."

My stomach lurches in both pleasure and anticipation, but my hands come up to scratch at his, my legs kicking backwards, playfully fighting him even when I want him to win, to dominate me, to *take* me.

He doesn't flinch, his grip on my neck tightening until I'm rendered still by the threat of strangulation. His teeth scrape over my pulse, making me shiver. "Fight me. That's good. Prey shouldn't concede."

Contradicting his words, he releases me abruptly and spins me around. He's a blur as he bends and hoists me over his shoulder, one arm tight around my waist. I have no idea where he's taking me, but right now, I couldn't care less.

His hand is heavy on my thigh, a threat on its own. My stomach continuously bounces against his shoulder. Up close, I examine exactly who I've been running from, and how impossibly big he is with muscles that make lifting me seem effortless. In this way, he reminds me of Jace again, and the image of him sitting across from me at the diner momentarily takes over.

When my stomach twists again, it's with a sense of guilt, but it's nudged aside when my hunter flips me right way up, pushing me against a tree. He reaches into his chest pocket, and that's when I notice the back of his hand. What I see makes me blink a few times, convinced I'm imagining it.

A scar.

A scar in the exact place I know Jace's to be.

There's no fucking way...

My gaze darts to his, searching through the mask for eyes that stalked me through work this week. Sat on my couch and listened to my baggage. The same eyes I thought I recognized earlier. He's not looking at me, though, so it's difficult to make anything out.

His hand comes between us, a metal sliding on metal noise dropping my attention to the item he's holding.

A knife.

A knife he strokes down the side of my face, sharpened edge away from my skin, tracing the line of my jaw. My breath hitches once he reaches my mouth.

His grin is a bit maniacal, and I study it, seeking Jace. Studying his jaw and cheek and stubble, looking for any hint of the man I've become reacquainted with.

The blade slides down my neck and over my clavicle, tracing the edge of my sweater. He hasn't hurt me, nor do I think he will, so I'm laying my limited trust in the hands of a stranger, hoping my body won't be found chopped up in a few hours.

He pauses his exploration to unzip my sweater, guiding it off my shoulders and letting it pool on the ground. The cool, nighttime breeze typical of late April brushes over my bare arms and stomach. I'm left with only a tight sports bra covering my chest.

He drags the knife down my stomach. Out of some unhealthy habit left over from Aaron's cruel comments, I suck in.

With a noise of displeasure, he taps the knife handle against my stomach. "Don't hide from me. *Every* part of you is beautiful, and I plan on tasting all of you."

I inhale sharply, this time not trapping any air in my lungs as he withdraws the knife, his dark eyes glistening with mischief—a warning we're about to play for real. He moves too quickly for me to catch another glimpse of his hand so I can know whether I'm insane and seeing things that aren't there.

He crouches and cuts off my pants, which actually irritates me because they cost a lot. I want to say something, but his actions hold too much allure in them for me to end this. My heartbeat hasn't slowed, despite the run having ended. Now, it's being elevated by my hunter.

He removes my shoes, and socks as well. Once they're discarded by my feet, he stands. Once more, I find myself checking his hand while asking myself the most important question: would I stop this regardless of whether he is Jace?

No. No, I wouldn't.

His fingers pinch my chin to angle my face up, turning me this way and that as he inspects my features. "Prove you've read my note. What are your safe words?"

"Amber to slow down, and golden to stop."

He nods once, a strange break after the intensity so far. It allows me to catch my breath, which I suspect will be needed for what's to come.

"Remember those. I won't hurt you anymore than you want to be, but if things go too far, use them. You've established I'm no serial killer. I'm also not a rapist. The words are there for a reason and will be respected."

I can do nothing but nod; the man steals all sensibilities. It only lasts a moment, because with his final comment, something passes over the little bit of his face I can make out. His jaw rotates forwards and he steps back, inspecting me standing in nothing more than panties and my sports bra, skin pebbling beneath the chill.

"Beautiful," he whispers reverently, his voice much too low to make out the similarities—if any—to Jace's.

He flips the knife before placing the blade, sharp edge out, between his teeth, and I swear I'm about to die and go to the afterlife, right here and now. The image of his mouth wrapped around a blade, a mask concealing the parts of him I may or may not be familiar with, as he stands fully dressed is a vision of pure sin I long to lose myself in. I'm not religious by any means, but if my hunter were a religion on his own, I'd worship him until my death.

His fingers trail over my stomach before slipping beneath the edge of my sports bra, and I remain perfectly still as he yanks it above my head, attention zeroing in on my budded nipples. He makes a low noise in his throat, then abruptly flips me so my chest scrapes against the rough bark of the tree, pulling a gasp from my throat. I'm rendered useless, caught between fight and flight, if not a bit confused, because this is more than anything I ever fantasized.

"Can't have you trying to escape, now can we?" Warm breath blows over my nape as he leans closer and tugs the bra into place, partway up my forearms. He releases me for a second before stabbing the knife through my bra, securing me to the tree. I'm now completely at his mercy.

Oh.

His hands trail down my arms and over my shoulders, pausing to cup my breasts before continuing to rest on my hips. He leans closer, the plastic of the mask dragging over my neck before his teeth imbed themselves in my shoulder. He chuckles darkly before his fingers find my panties, pushing them down my legs and discarding them to the side—a pink stain on the ground, evidence of our debauchery.

He steps back, allowing the cool air to pass between us, pebbling every inch now bare beneath the intensity of his gaze. While I may not be able to see him, I know he's staring. His eyes sweep over my legs, ass, and my back.

It's similar to the feeling I had when Jace pulled me between his legs the other night.

"You know what predators do when they catch their prey?"

My breath catches, and I shake my head, my tongue feeling too thick to form some comprehensible answer.

"They eat them."

SEVENTEEN
JACE

FUCK ME, isn't she the prettiest little meal.

Ripe and feral, her chest heaving. And we haven't even begun yet.

She's perfect.

If she were anyone else, I'd already be inside her. Others never put up such a solid effort. With them, it was all about the endgame. With Payton, though, I crave it all. I'll keep her here all night until we're satisfied, and if we never reach that point... Well, then I guess she's mine for good.

She has no idea what she's doing to me as she stands stuck to the tree, thanks to the switchblade stabbed into her bra. Her ass is round, and I can't wait to get my hands on her. Her thighs are nice and thick, rubbing against one another every few seconds as the anticipation builds within my terse silence.

As much as I long to bury myself inside her, I'll be damned if I don't get the Easter treat I've dreamed of for years.

I step close, trailing a finger down her spine, pleased when she shivers and arches. The bark will be rough on her skin, claiming their own bites like the ones I plan on decorating her with. I can't be gentle with her, but I won't hurt her. Nothing more than my girl can take, anyway.

When the rest of town attends church for Easter service tomorrow morning, I'll be recalling this moment. When I drop to my knees behind her and grasp her thighs, it solidifies this moment into my memory forever. My fingers dig into her flesh, my own personal altar I'll be praying to all night long until I'm filled with repentance. Her, my deity, the only one who'll own my loyalty.

I nudge her legs apart and tilt her hips, forcing her breasts against the tree. She makes a surprised noise, but utters no safe word, so I lean forwards and scrape my chin against her core, my day's scruff pulling forth a gasp.

"You make the best noises." My throat burns from trying to deepen my voice so she doesn't recognize me, but thankfully, I don't plan on speaking much more. "Cry for me," I add seconds before I *feast*.

My tongue swipes over her once before shoving as deep inside her as I can while my thumbs keep her spread. This second of tenderness is all I grant before hoisting one leg up and to the side, opening her wider.

She staggers slightly, the bra around her forearms keeping her upright. My teeth scrape over her clit, and she lurches against her restraints. I bite down, just hard enough to earn another breathy gasp.

"Jesus fucking Christ," she cries.

"Jesus forsakes people like you and me. He views this as a sin, whereas I can imagine no better place to pray to."

She moans, and I alternate between fucking her with my tongue and nipping her clit, her pussy, her thighs. The sight of my claiming bites unleashes a depraved side of me, and I sink my teeth in, leaving subtle indents no other fucker will ever be close enough to see. There's a sick thrill in knowing tonight will end with her marked by *me*.

I lean my face forwards to nip her clit again before petting her with my tongue, my hands massaging her ass as I rock her atop my face. She's between pleasure and pain, for every breathy moan is matched by a gasp when I peck. She struggles against her binds, pulling on the blade stabbed deep into the wood. As her orgasm approaches, her body alternates between arching into my mouth and trying to escape my hold, the pressure and high climbing within her. She's going to come soon. She's going to sate the thirst I've had for years.

"I-I'm..." She trails off, her hair brushing my hands as her head falls back. I can't see exactly what she's doing, nor will I be pulling away from my place of worship to check.

My thumbs massage her inner thighs as my licks get fevered—primal. Her noises grow louder, her head falling forwards this time as she cries out her orgasm, her juices coating my tongue in the most delicious flavour—musky and sweet, enhanced with all the excitement of the night.

I could happily bring her to orgasm with my mouth a few more times, but I'll be damned if she gets too sensitive before I'm inside her.

As she's gasping for breath, I lower her leg and retrieve my knife from above, freeing her. She falls against the tree, limp, but I catch her and turn her around, searching for signs of overstimulation.

Her gaze is hazy, and she's so fucking beautiful it knocks the wind out of me. Her chest is red, rubbed raw from the bark, and her hair is lightly tangled from the breeze.

"Good?" I check, taking a momentary pause for her well-being. Only when she nods do I move her away and shove her to her hands and knees.

My cock twitches to finally be released, and seeing her like this—her face tipped up, full, pouty lips practically begging for my cock, and breasts full—my hands ache to touch her again. Her eyes remain on mine, and it's almost unnerving how much it seems like she *sees* me. She doesn't, because with the lack of light and the mask, I'm well hidden.

"Spread your legs."

She inches them apart without argument.

"Do you feel my claim on you?"

Her lips twitch with a partial smirk, but she continues obeying, brushing her fingertips along my bite marks. She pets them gently, reverently.

"You liked that? Being eaten? Bitten?"

"Yes," she breathes, her pupils dilating in excitement.

"Good, because I'm nowhere close to being finished. Here." I rest my palm along her neck, over her pulse. "And here"—I cup her breasts —"will wear my claim."

The thought of biting her again makes my cock push against my zipper, begging to be set free and buried in our captive. She watches me undo myself, her head tipping slightly to the side, lips parting.

I'm working at the zipper when her attention suddenly darts away. Mischievousness passes over her face seconds before her plan formulates, hitting me the same instance she lunges to her feet.

So that's how she wants to play. *Oh, little rabbit, you've really fucked up this time.*

EIGHTEEN
PAYTON

I HAVE no idea why I ran again, especially when understanding the thrill of being caught. The orgasm against the tree was like none I've ever experienced before. It was a special kind of power, being pulled to the brink and shoved off the edge beneath the influence of the moon. Doing so in the woods is primal in itself, among the animals and nature that live without laws.

Lawless and free.

But the game goes on, because it's too thrilling not to. To provoke him, to force him to dominate me. Imagining what he's about to do makes me excited, because he won't let me go far. Nor do I really want to; just far enough to make my point.

Jace is chasing me. *Jace.*

It must be. When he was undoing his pants, it gave me a clear-as-day view of the scar. It's the same colour, shape, and size. Same hand.

The man in the wolf mask, who set this game up, is Jace. Which means—I can't even think about what it means.

Sticks stab into my bare feet, slowing me down. He's close, and I've probably only made it a dozen or so strides before his arms wrap around my waist and he forces us to the ground. My hands land on the earth, twigs digging in.

He's rough when he kicks my legs apart and reaches for my arms, wrenching them behind my back and pinning them together in one hand. My chest is pushed into the ground, dirt and leaves tangling in my hair. With his other hand, he yanks my knotted locks, lifting my head backwards, then bends over, the outline of his cock pressing against my ass.

"Nice try, but not again. Realize this now—no matter how far you run, I'll be a step ahead. No matter how hard you fight, I'll be stronger. If you do that again, I'll make your ass so red, you won't be able to sit until next Easter."

I squirm despite his warning, but all it does is rub my ass against him. He's doing a really damn good job of masking his voice, but now I hear what my mind didn't put together before this. It's there: the same roughness as Jace's.

He pauses like he's thinking about something, then abruptly releases me to stand, hauling me to my knees. I'm a ragdoll for him to control as he finishes what he began before I darted off. He undoes his pants, the zipper loud in the forest's silence.

His hand delves into my hair, his other gripping his now-freed cock. He's hard, the tip glistening with pre-cum, and I find myself licking my bottom lip, imagining the taste.

He groans, gripping my hair tighter as he hauls me closer. "Been dreaming of this mouth since the moment I saw you, little rabbit. You thought to run, so you get to pay the price. Open."

My lips part, and he guides my head closer, the tip of him kissing my lips seconds before my next inhale. He takes that opportunity to thrust deep, hitting the back of my throat and immediately causing me to gag, my reflexes not having caught up yet.

He pulls back halfway, murmuring, "Tap my leg in place of your safe words. One tap for amber, and two for golden."

It's his one moment of kindness, because then he places both hands around my head and pushes me onto him, roughly fucking my face. It's animalistic and delicious, all wrapped up in debauchery. He controls everything from the speed to the depth, my mouth nothing more than a wet hole for him to fuck. My tongue drags along the underside of his cock, trying my best to brush the sensitive part of him and have *some* power in this.

"You have no fuckin' idea how sexy you look on your knees, sucking my cock. A view I could come from."

Spit gathers in my mouth, his speed not allowing me to swallow, and the act fills the forest with a sound so depraved, so erotic, my pussy clenches around nothing, anticipating him being inside me. His moans pierce the air, telling me while he's rendered me immobilized, I'm far from powerless.

He abruptly pulls from my mouth with a curse, his thumb coming down on my bottom lip as he forces my mouth open. "To see my cum in here...next time, perhaps."

Will there be a next time? Fuck, I hope so.

He places me back on my hands and knees, the same position he put me in after catching me, and grabs my arms, pulling them behind my body until my torso kisses the ground.

"Don't you dare move them," he demands, so I don't, holding my elbows still until my body is half numb. He grasps my hair, looping it around a fist and tugging lightly.

The head of his cock rubs over my clit. "I have a condom. Will I need one?"

I shake my head as much as his hold allows for. "I'm safe and on birth control."

He strokes over me before pushing inside, sinking three inches deep before pausing, and then seating himself another three inches with a loud groan. The hold he has on my hair tightens until my scalp screams. It causes my back to arch, making my pussy clamp tighter, my nipples rubbing painfully against the ground.

Fuck, this position is everything.

Then he moves, and I die.

My hands falter on my back, but he's right there, clamping his free one over them to keep me in position.

"When rabbits are caught in snares, they're not given freedom. You won't be going anywhere until you're full of my cum."

I whimper, unable to hold in the pathetic sound. No one's made me feel like this before. Not Aaron, that's for certain. This is Jace. And I don't know what to think. What happens when I have to look him in the face tomorrow and pretend tonight never happened?

"When your pussy is dripping with cum, that's when I'll let you go. I'll let you run as far as your legs will take you while hunting you again. After this, no one else will touch you, not when you're so deeply imprinted with me."

He thrusts into me so hard, his statement engraves on my insides. I'll have marks tomorrow for sure, but I'll cherish every damn one. The external ones from the ground and his grip, and the internal ones on how his claim affects my emotions.

He releases my wrists, not complaining when I lower them to the ground. Even with them free, I'm rendered useless by the grip he maintains on my hair, tilting me as he shifts, changing the angle of his cock inside me.

He suddenly releases my hair, and then his fingers are coming around the front of my neck until they brush against my pulse. In this position, my life is literally in the palm of his hands, but he's an executioner I'm more than willing to kneel for.

He uses my throat to propel me onto my knees, my back against his front. He tips my head to the side to bare my neck to him. As his thrusts quicken, taking me to the edge, he sinks his teeth in. In his hold, my orgasm lets loose. When he comes, he doesn't yell out, just bites harder as heat shoots deep inside me, his claim officially laid.

After a moment and many sharp inhales, he slips out of me and gently lowers my body to the ground, coming down on top of me. His breaths vibrate through my chest, and I match mine to his.

To Jace's.

He feels *really* good.

Much too soon, and with a sigh indicating we're sharing the same feelings, he lifts off. His hands massage my back, ass, and thighs. "You okay?" His voice slipped ever so slightly there, losing some of the gruff.

"Perfect."

A forest floor should never be this comfortable, but beneath his caresses, I could sleep here. Minutes pass before he stands and does up his pants before retrieving mine, half of them in ruins. Inside my sweater, the Easter egg is still hidden, and I wonder if he knows I found one. I'm not sure I even have it in me to cash it in, considering tonight's already been everything I imagined.

He rests my clothing on my chest before sliding one arm behind my back, the other going beneath my legs. He lifts me with little effort, then starts walking.

"Where are you taking me?"

"Your house," he says in an almost insulted tone.

"You carry all your women?" I roll my head to study the parts of his face unhidden by the mask, like the line of his jaw, searching for more clues I'm not delusional in thinking this man is Jace. The scar is pretty damning, though...

"No." His reply is short, if not a bit tainted by dismay.

We near the edge of the woods much too quickly. Whyever Jace did this, I want to thank him. This night was more than I ever imagined, and knowing it was with someone trustworthy made it better. I wasn't sold on the idea of fucking a stranger, even if I believed him to be Jace when deciding not to return the golden egg outside.

Still, to imagine next time I see him, I'll have to pretend not to know what he feels like inside me. How his hands feel caressing my skin, his tongue on my clit. It's impossible; I'll combust after a greeting.

When I expect him to drop me on my porch, he strides up the two steps and heads for the door. "Door unlocked?"

"Yeah."

He shuffles me in his arms to free a hand to twist the knob, using his hip to nudge it open the rest of the way. He kicks it shut before carrying me down the hallway and into my bedroom—all without direction, which suggests he's been watching me. Something that should be petrifying, but isn't.

Well, that answers the question of who was watching me the other night. The next day was when I first saw Jace after the eight-year gap. It all makes sense.

He grabs my clothes from where they still rest on my chest and drops them onto the floor before pulling back the comforter and sliding me beneath it. Aches I never could have imagined come to attention at the change in position. Too soon, my limbs melt into the mattress, my head hazy with exhaustion.

He stares down at me, his hands forming fists by his sides. He uncurls and reforms them twice before his tongue dabs at his lower lip, seeming like there's more he wants to say. And maybe he does. Maybe he wants to admit his identity in the same way I want to tell him I'm aware.

Instead, his fingers linger on my arm, lightly tracing, before he pulls away with obvious resistance. Before he gets too far, I reach for his hand—the scarred one—and link my fingers with his, tugging him into a kneeling position beside the bed.

This time, he's caught in my snare, body still as he watches me trace up his arm, over his shoulder, and across his jaw near the ribbon tied behind his head holding his mask on.

But I don't tug the ribbon, not willing to reveal what we both know. Instead, I drag my nails through his hair, giving him even an ounce of the pleasure he granted me tonight.

"My ex-boyfriend broke up with me for that reason. Well, it was one of a few reasons, anyway. He wasn't interested in my fantasies, so thank you for making them come true." Facts Jace knows, but I'm feigning oblivion.

"Your ex didn't deserve you." More hints of my Jace emerge in the sharpness of his tone, his age-old loathing for Aaron peeking through. "Some people aren't compatible. You'll have to find that one."

Like you.

"Compatibility wasn't our only issue. He blamed everything on me, not only sex. When life started to get busy and we couldn't spend every waking minute together, he got annoyed. When university got demanding, he complained I wasn't being a good girlfriend. When wanting to experiment in the bedroom, he called me sick. When bills piled up because, despite his parents funding his life, he contributed very little, I became stressed and my body changed. He didn't like that either."

I don't really know why I say all this, considering it's nothing Jace doesn't know already. But he doesn't know I know, so acting the part is key before this night blows up in awkwardness.

Dark eyes stroke down my skin. "I love every inch of your body. He's a fool. You've become my Easter treat, my place of worship, my sin on earth."

His words bring the hint of a smile to my face, enough to remind me of all the positive mindset changes I had to go through after my breakup with Aaron.

"Why did you tell me that?" he asks after a moment.

"Because you're the only one who's made me feel better." *Now and then. You as my hunter, and as Jace.*

From down the hallway, Aaron's notes are once again a beacon. A part of me wants to tell him, knowing he's Jace, because he'll *care*. But considering he's supposed to be anonymous and there's technically nothing between us, it wouldn't be right pulling him into my drama more than he already has been.

He grabs my hand in response, bringing the tips of my fingers to his teeth then lightly nipping, reminding me once again of the love bites decorating my thighs.

I want more before he goes.

I inch closer, turning until my thighs fall on either side of his body. He doesn't stop me when I tug him closer, nor when I tip my head up and brush his lips with my own. He freezes as both past and present catch up to two old friends.

Suddenly, both my hands are in his, and he climbs half on top of me, kissing me harder, sweeping me away and back to places only reached on a primal level. His tongue traces the seam of my mouth, and I part my lips to let him in.

His kiss is a fevered promise of more while also being a resigned goodbye.

Too soon, he pulls away and releases my hands. His lips press together as though to lock the taste of me into him—at least, that's what I tell myself—and he traces a line down my cheek.

"I never stay," he says suddenly. "Anyone I've done this with in the past, after making sure they're good and dressed, I don't carry them home. I don't tuck them in. I *never* kiss them."

"Glad I'm your first."

His lips twitch into a sad, almost smile, and then his touch is completely gone as he turns for the door. His reply is a whisper, something more for me than him.

"You've always been my first, Payton."

And then he's gone, and a few moments later, my front door shuts.

NINETEEN

JACE

EASTER SUNDAY COMES, and I drag my ass out of bed to attend the town's egg hunt, only so I can see her.

Her. Payton. A fucking religion of the highest order. A deity who owns my heart, soul, and loyalty. If last night was considered a sin, then I'll burn in Hell to do it with her again.

I want to make sure she's okay, but I can't ask.

I want to look at her and know the marks are from me.

I want to see how she reacts around me, how much of her recent sexual history she'll pretend doesn't exist.

After three coffees, I dress and leave, throwing my hat on to hide the black smudges beneath my eyes. I got maybe an hour of sleep after returning from Payton's, only leaving once her lights shut off.

I tasted her. Fucked her. Touched her. Kissed her.

I need so much more. As me, not as a stranger in the night. I want her aware of who's been inside her.

Years of fantasies came true last night, and I'll be damned if it takes that long for a repeat.

I drive downtown, finding a parking spot around the corner from Fawn's Diner. Cars line most of the side roads, because it seems the town doubles in capacity for events since everyone and their dog (literally) comes out for them.

I scan the town's centre—a small piece of land in front of the mayor's office and a town hall most often used for events and gatherings. Some hundreds of people are already mingling, kids vibrating with excitement.

At the front, the mayor and his wife—Bennett's parents—are giving an introductory speech about Easter and family time and other bullshit I tune out, searching for Payton, and even Bennett. If his parents are here, no doubt he's looming, and I'll lose my shit if he says anything degrading to her. Or really, anything at all.

A hand clamps on my shoulder, jerking my attention to Brad and his wife, Claire, coming to stand beside me. Claire's hand is resting on the side of her large bump.

"Hey," I greet them. "You okay there? Should I keep my truck nearby in case a hospital run is required?"

She rolls her eyes, tapping her pregnant belly. "Still three to four months to go. I'll be fine."

Brad shoulders me. "Surprised to see you here."

"Yeah, well, I…" Don't really have a reason for attending, considering every annual egg hunt—along with most town celebrations, for that matter—I avoid.

"I meant"—Brad twists me around—"I'm surprised you're standing here when Payton's over there." He points through the crowd.

Across the field, Payton's listening to the mayor's speech. Her hands are shoved in the pockets of a maroon-coloured coat that dips past her hips. Her hair's done up away from her face, and she's speaking with a woman beside her. I recognize her from around town as one of the few to ever relocate here, rather than have familial connections to these parts. Gwen is her name, I believe.

Barely remembering I'm beside two friends, I wave bye and head for Payton, cutting through the crowd until I'm in front of her, ending whatever conversation she and Gwen were having.

Payton pauses, staring up at me, and I search for any sign she has a clue I'm the one she was with last night. But her eyes remain bright, shining in the afternoon sun, trusting though cautious—the norm for how she's always regarded me. Up close, the marks on her neck are apparent, unhidden behind embarrassment, and something inside me roars. Now, I *hope* Bennett's around so he understands she's moved on and has reclaimed that part of herself.

"Hey," she greets, teeth sliding over her bottom lip, and I'm taken back to last night when she did the same thing before I secured her to the tree.

"Hey. Happy Easter. Here for the hunt?" *Obviously she is, dumbass.*

Her friend offers her hand to shake. "Hey, name's Gwen. Don't think I've ever had the pleasure. You run the construction company in town, right?"

"That'd be me. Name's Jace." I adjust my hat, which has my company's logo etched onto it, and return my attention to the woman who invaded my entire night—senses, brain, and every breath since eight p.m.

"Yeah." Payton shifts, glancing past me as the crowd begins breaking apart. "Don't really want to be here, but Gwen insisted."

"It's good for you to get out of the house and diner once in a while." Gwen knocks into her shoulder, throwing a sly grin my way. "Wouldn't you agree, Jace?"

Am I supposed to say yes?

"Then again," Gwen continues, "Payton's recently taken up long walks in the forest, so I guess that counts."

I stiffen, and so does Payton.

"We should get going," Payton mumbles, stepping back.

Gwen follows, but quickly retrieves her phone out with an

annoyed groan. "My mom's calling. I need to take this, sorry. But you two are good, right?" Her attention flicks between us. Without waiting for a response, she takes off in the opposite direction without answering her phone, which I'm guessing wasn't actually ringing.

"She's not subtle, is she?" Payton stares at her friend walking away with a head shake. "Either way, we should get going."

The field is mostly empty, small families and groups spreading throughout town. Already, kids are shouting in excitement as they discover coloured eggs behind bushes and on store ledges.

Payton leads me down the closest road, waiting until we're farther away from people. Being beside her is near impossible, making me wonder how I believed I'd manage this all day. As the wind picks up her hair, it reminds me of when it was streaming behind her as she ran last night.

"You look tired." She glances up at me, lingering on the bags beneath my eyes.

"Didn't sleep well."

"Exciting night?"

"Something like that," I answer carefully, searching her expression for any indication why she cares.

Payton glances over her shoulder before taking a side street out of view. A few steps down, she abruptly turns, pulling her hand from her pocket.

In her palm is one of my eggs from last night she didn't cash in.

Fuck. Maybe? I don't know what the hell it means.

"Found one before the hunt began? Impressive." I go with a lie, because my rapid heart isn't certain what to say.

"Don't play dumb, Jace. I know it was you last night."

Shit.

Her expression remains calm and collected, but there's no doubt at any moment, she's about to be pissed I technically lied and broke her trust, meeting up with her as a stranger rather than admitting who was beneath the mask.

"How'd you figure it out?"

"Your scar." She flicks her eyes toward my hand, which fists in response. "I first noticed it after you caught me, and thought I was seeing things. Between the quick movements and concealing your voice, I couldn't be certain until you began undoing your pants."

When I had her on her knees in front of me, a sight that'll live rent-free in my head.

There's a fact buried within her words. A fact that shoots a lightning bolt to my senses.

She knew *before* I fucked her, which means she was with *me* willingly.

"I'm not mad," she murmurs, her admittance damning us both further. "It was better knowing it was you. I'm glad it was."

Fucking Christ, she's going to unravel me.

"I could have stopped you any time," she continues. "At first, you were the stranger I so unwisely hoped wouldn't be a murderer. Once you caught me and I figured it out, everything made more sense. If anything, thank you. After my house, you kinda acted differently, and I assumed it was something I said. That, like Aaron, I freaked you out and lost my only remaining non-friend—"

I shut her up, unable to take another fucking word.

Her back hits the brick wall behind us as I haul her face to mine, kissing her with everything I am and everything I want to be for her. It's different than last night, when I was cautious and afraid she'd go for my mask. This time, I'm kissing her as *me*.

My hands cup her face, fingers brushing along the marks on her neck. It's with a low, pleased moan I tip her head to the side and drag my lips over them, reminding us both what they mean.

"You didn't freak me out. I left because I had to stop myself from doing this." I nip her pulse, pushing my body against hers. "Never compare me to Bennett, because the moment I act like him is the moment I want you to take a hammer to my head." I lift off her, catching her gaze to make her see the sincerity in my words. "Never let me be like that dick. Never let me hurt you, no matter what. As long as I'm not like him, I promise, little rabbit, you'll never lose me."

Her hand comes up to my face, thumb dragging across my bottom lip. "'Little rabbit.' I don't know how I didn't hear it the first time, since the similarities in your voice are *all* I can hear now."

I nip her thumb with my teeth. "Also, I'm not your non-friend, Payton. We were kidding ourselves giving it that title."

"Then what are you? What are we?"

"Whatever you want us to be."

Her eyes drop to my chest as her hand skates down my front, pausing over where my heart lies. She seems to think it through, but never grants me the answer I long for.

"Thank you," she whispers after a moment. "For doing all that. *Being* that. The knife, the running...it's what I wanted."

"What you *needed*." I tip her chin up with a finger, brushing my lips over hers.

She brings the egg from last night between us, holding it up. "This thing still get me what I want?"

"Consider me the Easter Bunny. Or a genie."

"Can I instead consider you a wolf again? That's what I want: a repeat. Tonight. This time as you. No mask. I want to look behind me and see *you*."

Always.

"Get running, little rabbit." I grab the egg from her, slipping it into my pocket as I lay a final lick to the inside of her wrist. "Sundown tonight, I'll be coming."

WHEN EVENING FALLS, I'm all but a waiting mess.

Eventually, I go outside and settle on the steps, drawing my legs up to my chest to stay warm as the final dredges of sunlight disappear into the treeline. With nightfall, a figure emerges from the shadows, and my body is met with a visceral reaction, urging me to my feet.

His hood is drawn up, so I can't make out his face. There's no wolf mask—that much is noticeable. He takes a single step forward, and my blood ignites as I skip down the stairs and into the woods.

We didn't come up with a plan, so I don't know if he'll be giving me a head start this time, but not knowing is an additional thrill. There's no rules this time. No prep. Just him and me and the woods.

My feet kick up dirt and sticks in my mad rush into the forest, but his heavy steps are fast approaching. *Damn, he's not playing tonight.* It's almost disappointing he's ending this so soon, but after experiencing Jace intimately last night, I'm sure getting caught will be all kinds of vicious fun.

He's quicker than yesterday, and his hand snatches the back of my shirt, yanking me to a stop. It pulls against my neck, strangling me; rough in all the wrong ways—my first hint something isn't right.

My back is slammed to the ground and, even as my arms come up to fight, he pins them with his knees, settling on top of me. His weight digs in painfully, and it's too much.

This isn't like last night. It feels wrong.

"G-golden." The safe word should end this.

He doesn't get off me. The figure tips his head back, revealing his face at the same time he speaks, his voice straight from my nightmarish past.

"I fuckin' warned you, you little slut. Warned you what would happen if you fucked someone else. You're mine, whether you want to believe it or not."

Aaron.

My hips and legs kick wildly to get him off, to free my hands for some kind of fighting chance, but his weight easily overpowers me. I attempt to readjust my legs between his, hoping my knee can land in the one area that never quite held up.

"You shouldn't have bankrupted me, cheated on me, emotionally abused me—shall I continue? You stopped deserving me eight years ago."

"And you," he pushes down harder, "shouldn't have fucked another man. Enjoy yourself last night, whore?"

He was here? Watching? The knowledge he witnessed the best night of my life causes bile to rise in my throat

"Yeah." He grins. "Came by last night so we could talk, but then I saw something so interesting. I watched you taking off into the forest before some asshole followed you, *found* you." He sneers. "And you rolled right over and took it, didn't you?"

I could only imagine what kind of "talking" he wanted to do.

"Knowing what I like in bed doesn't make me a whore."

He snorts. "Except you don't like fucking in a bed, do you?" He readjusts, swinging one leg over my hip and pushing his pelvis down into me, his belt buckle digging into my waistband, a threat on its own.

But it's a threat I'm done listening to. "If this is what you want, to be fucked like an animal in the dirt, then it's what I'll give you. Punishment for spreading your legs for another man when you're *mine*."

He reaches for his belt, giving me the slim room to wiggle my leg between us and ram my knee straight up into his balls.

He howls and rolls to the ground, clutching himself, and I don't wait around. Scrambling to my hands and knees, I bolt for home, but my plan is to continue past it and screech for the neighbours' attention, who live way down the road. Anyone who'll hear me and call one of the few asshole cops this town has. They'll probably take Aaron's side —again—but it'll be enough of a deterrent for tonight.

I make it twenty feet before he bellows, but I skip checking to see if he's following. Pumping my arms faster than I believed possible, I keep going, because this isn't a game like last night. This is real, shitty life. The reality of being a woman once overpowered by a man for so many years, but I'm done being that person.

Done being scared. Done being anxious. Done hiding my desires.

Finally, when I feel far enough away to check if he's in pursuit, I do. My hair whips in front of my face, but I don't slow, tearing it from my vision without enough time to notice the large form I slam face-first into before it's too late.

Hands cup my shoulders, forcing me still, but I fight. Screeching and hitting, I don't think about the fact Aaron is somewhere behind me, not holding me.

"Payton—hey! Payton." Warmth encompasses my cheek, forcing my face upward to meet the eyes of a storm, and I'm immediately swept away by the water. "Little rabbit, what's wrong?" He takes in my dishevelled appearance, my tangled hair, and the fact my limbs are quivering. Fear and adrenaline catch up now that I'm with someone who'll never hurt me, and all I can do is point.

He follows my finger right as Aaron emerges from the trees, his steps staggered and slow, face paler than before.

"He...he attacked—I tried. I got away..." My arm falls limp by my side, and Jace takes it, sliding me behind him. His body is taut, poised, as he stares daggers at Aaron.

His jaw is all hard lines and cracked stone when he utters, "Get home. Lock your door. Don't answer for anyone but me. I'll take care of this."

He takes a step, and my heart lurches, because I don't know what he'll do. His face is empty and lifeless. Murderous. I've never seen him like this before.

"Don't kill him." I reach for Jace's hand. My touch skates over his scar, the mark that initially connected me to him. "He's not worth going to prison for."

"No, but you are."

"Jace—"

"I won't kill him," he promises. "I just found you. You won't be getting rid of me. Go back to the house."

THERE ARE VERY few things that have ever caused me to feel true fear, but finding Payton running through the woods without me chasing her tops the list.

When I arrived at her house, immediately something felt off. She wasn't waiting inside or out, and I didn't believe she'd leave early. A strange instinct pulled me into the forest and right to her.

I should have fucking guessed Bennett was involved in her disappearance.

Once Payton's safely out of view, I glare at the prick who's still not walking quite right. When I'm done with him, he'll be nothing more than scraps for the animals to pick at.

"Shouldn't surprise me *you're* the one fucking her."

I'm not a murderer, but everyone is capable of it, no matter what lies they tell themselves. Perhaps it's ironic—on the weekend meant for repenting one's sins, I'm fantasizing about committing the ultimate one.

If there's anyone I'd go to jail for, it's her. To ensure her well-being, and that he's unable to breathe near her. She's worth the first-degree murder charge, but being without her is another thing entirely.

Like I reassured her, I'm not ready to let her go after finally finding her.

So, I won't. Doesn't mean I'll go easy on him, though.

His staggered steps are slow, so I meet him halfway, grasping his shirt like I did the other day in the diner. He swings at my face, which is easy to duck, and his half-assed attempt lands in my stomach. I block his next incoming punch, then stick a foot out so he trips, landing on the ground.

I come down on top of him, my fists saying what the blood roaring through my ears longs to. He blocks every few, but his attempts are getting weaker and weaker. Before I accidentally kill him, the possessive feeling controlling me needs to be reeled in.

Blood streams from his nose and into his mouth, and his eyes are more glazed than before. His face already shows hints of the swelling and bruises he'll wear later.

"Now that you're listening, listen well. Leave town. Do not contact her. Do not look at her. Do not even *think* about her."

He spits, blood splattering onto my face. "You can't do shit to me, Hayes. But I—"

Hands in his shirt, I haul him upright. My teeth clamp together, making my next words gritted. "Test me and see what happens. *She* is the only reason you're still breathing, so be fuckin' thankful I honour my promises to her. Piss me off again, and I'll bury you alive in my cement truck. It'd be a pretty shit way to go, don't ya think?"

Blood drains from his face.

"You know my demands. The money you charged to her cards and the bankruptcy you put her in will be cleared. You and I both know Mommy's and Daddy's bank accounts are well padded, and there wasn't a need to exploit her. By noon tomorrow, you'll repay every last cent you owe her with ten percent interest. Don't, and you and I will be taking a little drive in my cement truck. You won't enjoy the destination, but it'll be a peaceful end to my holiday."

"You're fucked, man. Fucked in the head. She ain't worth it."

I release him, slowly unpeeling one finger at a time from his shirt. "That's where you're wrong. She *is* worth it. She's worth everything, but you always had your head up your ass." Pulling out my phone, I check the time. "You have seventeen hours, and that's more than enough time to get the money. Tick, tock, Bennett. By one p.m. tomorrow, I better see your car driving out of town."

I turn to leave. The only thing that stops me is his next question, ground out between a low, pained moan. "She tell you about the notes?"

Ice cools my veins. "What notes?"

He smirks. "Just the reminder she'll always be mine, no matter who she fucks."

If the bullshit he's spewing is true, Payton will be the one to tell me as soon as I make sure she's okay. Finished with this conversation and his bullshit, I tread close to him for a final time, ramming my heel into his ribs. The satisfying crack fills the air seconds before his scream.

Whatever notes there may or may not be, if he wrote them, then he deserves the injury.

I walk away, leaving him in misery.

PAYTON LEAPS UP from the couch when I enter, her gaze darting to my bloodied knuckles. She takes off down the hall, returning a moment later with a first-aid kit. Wordlessly, she begins cleaning my knuckles, her fingers quickly marred with Bennett's blood. The sight makes me rethink my cement truck plan, wanting to do it now.

"What happened?"

"Doesn't matter. He'll leave you alone. He'll also repay you all the money he spent, with interest."

She stares warily at the cuts on my hand with the scar that gave away my identity. It would be fitting if tonight creates another scar—both gave me her. "You didn't have to."

"Yeah, I did. I shouldn't have *had* to, though. That's the difference."

"It wasn't your responsibility."

"Payton." Unable to finish the statement without sounding maniacal, I grasp the back of her neck and tug her backwards with me, settling her on my lap. "*You're* my responsibility now, because it's what I want. Tell me about these notes he wrote you."

Her shoulders deflate with her murmured curse. With another sigh, she twists off my lap and leans toward the coffee table. Pulling open the drawer, she retrieves three scraps of paper and hands them to me.

I take them, reading them once. Twice. Then a few more times, each letter ingraining itself into me before I'm shooting off the couch, intending to hunt him down again.

"I shouldn't have left him alive."

"No!" She lunges, her small hands slipping around mine. "Don't do it. Don't let him ruin any more of our night."

This isn't about *ruining* a night; it's about the fucking fact he's been *threatening* her.

There's not enough ice in the world to cool my fury, making my next words gritted. "Payton, he's been threatening you. Why the fuck didn't you say anything?"

"I tried. I found the third note the day before you came to the diner. Before work that day, I brought them to the police, figuring maybe they could do something, like maybe help me file a restraining order. But they didn't believe me. They barely even *listened* to me."

Not surprising, considering his family connections.

"Honestly, at first I assumed he was just being mean. He never said anything 'til the diner the other day. Inside and out of it."

Out? My mind scrolls to that day, realization like a cold splash of water. The kick to Bennett's ribs better keep him out there long enough the animals pick him apart alive, because I swear to fucking—

"Before I picked you up," I confirm, already knowing the answer.

Her nod is barely a bob. "Said I was still his, and I shouldn't sleep with anyone else."

I'm sure there's more to it given the shit he said to me, but my sanity can only take so much.

"Why didn't you tell *me*? You didn't have to deal with this alone."

"I've been dealing with him alone for years. We were just getting friendly again, and I didn't want to ruin it."

I hate this. Hate it more than anything.

Payton tugs on my hand again, urging me back to the couch. "It's over, it's fine. Jace, let it go."

Let stalking and threats go? Un-fucking-likely.

"Fine," I lie, "but I'm keeping the notes."

She stares warily at where I'm gripping them. The question is clear in her expression, but it goes unasked.

After a tense moment of silence, she tugs on me again. "Shower with me? I'd really like to wash *him* off me."

The fact she needs to, coupled with the threats in my hand, reignite the murderous rage in my veins.

Tomorrow. He's tomorrow's problem.

"I hate he ruined our night," she mutters, leading me toward the bathroom.

"Night's far from ruined, little rabbit. We haven't tested your bed yet." I release her hand to scoop her into my arms. "Lucky for you, the egg is like a credit card. It'll retain my debt to you until you ask me to pay it off. We'll have a repeat of last night another day."

She doesn't reply, and I wonder if she's thinking about her own debt that will soon be paid off. She'll be free to do what she wants and to live where she wants.

I want her here with me.
Now that I have her, I won't let her go.

TWENTY-TWO

PAYTON

JACE IS GONE when I wake the next morning, my limbs still achy and sore from the other night. I prop myself up, pulling the blanket to my chest while searching for any sign he's still around, just not in the bedroom.

My search is interrupted by my phone ringing.

"Hello?"

A deep voice comes through the other end. "Miss Thorne?"

"Speaking."

"Good, hello. This is Officer Bennett. Would you be able to come down to the station to provide a statement?"

My gaze flicks one more to the empty space beside me, my stomach dropping. Of course, Aaron went to his uncle about last night, who, unsurprisingly, took his side again. Which means, Jace is in trouble. Trouble I did my damnedest to leave him out of.

"Can I ask what this is about?"

"Did you receive threats from a Mr. Aaron Bennett?"

The notes. Jace asked to keep them.

"Uh, yeah." *I told you this already, and you didn't listen.*

"Then we'll need your statement, if you'd please. Evidence was brought forward that matched Aaron's handwriting. When called upon, Aaron disclosed his written and verbal threats toward you."

"Oh, um. Wow. Okay, I'll be right down."

WHEN I MAKE IT OUTSIDE, Jace is pulling up in his truck. He backs in so the passenger side faces me, then lowers the window to talk.

"Figured you might need a drive."

"What did you do?" Despite everything, the smile plastered on my face since Aaron's uncle called hasn't died.

"Protected you in the most legal way I could by ensuring the law was upheld by the people who should have helped you a while ago. Wasn't that hard, really. A bit of shouting and thumping desks, and someone finally took me seriously. When they called in Aaron, bruises and all, he didn't put up too much of a fight before admitting everything. I was getting kicked out at that point, but I overheard them mentioning charges like attempted sexual assault, uttering threats, physical assault, and stalking. If it goes through, it should put him away for a while."

Aaron will be gone from my life. *Gone* gone. When I moved from Toronto to here, even before learning he followed me, I always knew pieces of him would linger. With him behind bars, he'll be out of my life for good with no trace except some bad memories.

I practically climb over the console to maul Jace, kissing my thanks into him twenty times over.

Maybe it's okay to let some people in.

MY STATEMENT IS TAKEN with little fanfare and is followed by an apology.

Aaron's parents are there, horrified when they learn what their son has done. The lawyer sitting with them is immediately dismissed when they choose not to fight the charges being pressed.

They trail me out of the station to where Jace is waiting beside his truck.

"I'm sorry," his mother says. "You were always too nice to him, even back then, but I'm sorry for the man he's become." She glances at her husband, her brows pulled tight. He nods in response to whatever silent conversation they're having before she reaches into her purse and pulls out a leather chequebook.

Flipping it open to the first blank cheque, she signs her name before handing it to me, along with the pen. "Please. Whatever he owes you, double it. Our apology for not only the spending, but everything else."

Double? Double clears my debt *and* resets my life.

I stare at the line, mentally calculating the number. "This isn't a bribe?" Aaron being out of my life is worth more than the debt. Debt I can and have been working off, but Aaron's threats...not so much.

"Not at all," his father rumbles. "The courts may charge our son with whatever they see fit. Hopefully, he'll learn his lesson. No, this money is because you didn't deserve any of this."

With their reassurance, I scribble down the number before showing them, almost asking permission to take this kind of cash.

Mrs. Bennett rips the cheque from the folder and hands it to me, her thin lips pulled into a meager smile before they walk away.

Jace comes up behind me, pulling me into his side. He's staring at the cheque with awe. "Damn."

"Right? I'm free."

"You're free until tonight. Then, you're all mine. Start running, little rabbit."

EPILOGUE

JACE

Two Months Later

BRAD SCANS the side of the newly constructed building, nodding in approval. "This looks awesome. Why do you look so fuckin' nervous? She'll love it."

"Or she'll hate it."

It's a worry that's been plaguing me since getting this idea. I've pushed construction on this project ahead of some of our contracts when time worked in my favour. Often, I'd return after hours, with Brad's assistance, to work as long as the sun cooperated. Thankfully, being mid-June, daylight has been on our side.

"Why would she?"

"She'll see it as me manipulating her to stay in town? Bennett took her choices away by forcing her to live in Toronto, then fucking her over. I don't want to be another guy who takes away her free will."

"Dude, she's still here, isn't she?"

"Yeah..."

It's been two months since Bennett's arrest and Payton getting the money. Every morning for the days following, I woke convinced I'd find her house packed and her gone.

But she never left, or mentioned the possibility. In case it's eventually coming, I've wasted no time, spending every waking second by her side. Just like our friendship never was titled as such, our relationship hasn't really been defined either. In my heart, though, I know she has the same kinds of feelings for me as I do her.

Brad slaps me on my shoulder, pulling me from my wandering thoughts. "She's off work soon, right? Pick her up and show her. She'll love it, I swear. And she won't run screaming. Now, speaking of screaming, Claire's been extra horny. Pregnancy hormones are nuts. So, gotta go."

"An image I didn't need, thanks." I wave him off, then turn back to the building that'll hopefully be the final piece to making Payton's dreams come true.

PAYTON

Five o'clock can't come fast enough. Jace messaged to tell me he has something important to show me, and while I can't imagine what it is, I'm excited to find out.

I wave goodbye to Jim and Fawn, then head out to where Jace's truck is idling by the curb, climbing in before giving him a kiss.

"Work went well?"

"Not bad." It's better now that I'm working to maintain an income, rather than chipping away at endless debt. Waitressing isn't my endgame career, but it's suitable for now.

Turns out, it was entirely Aaron and his actions keeping me from moving on. Since he's been taken care of, I've come to appreciate the small cabin turned home. After years in Toronto, I realized I adore this town. It's less stressful, there's no feeling of being rushed, and there's a fraction of the number of residents.

Then there's Jace. If I'm honest with myself, he's the entire reason I haven't left. I…like him. Maybe even more than like him, though sometimes it feels too soon to be thinking that way. But it's true, and going another eight years without him isn't possible.

Jace shifts in his seat four different times as he drives through town. He passes the bookstore and pizza joint, heading to the very end of a side street before parking in front of an empty building, its large windows overlooking a small field on the opposite side.

Jace slips out of the truck, then comes around the front to help me out. His hand is large around mine, and he positions me in front of the building before procuring a key from his pocket.

"What's this?"

"Yours, if you want it to be."

The single-storey building is mine? It's difficult to see through the slightly tinted windows, but what's clear is it's an empty space.

"Over the past month and a half, I've been building this from the ground up. The land was up for rent, so I got it. Those late nights I was working with Brad? This was it."

I still don't understand…

"I'm giving it to you, Payton, so you can open your vet practice." He lifts his hat and replaces it on his head: his nervous twitch. "The building's a done deal. I know starting up a business costs a lot, but I figure now that your debt is all paid, including your student loans with the extra money from the Bennetts, it won't be hard to get a business loan. Plus, the construction company's doing really well for itself, so I'd like to invest. Silent partner, of course. Really, I want nothing back." The ground between his feet apparently becomes very interesting since that's all he can look at, and he readjusts his hat once more. "I know you, so I know you won't take a freebie, even though that's what I'm asking you to do with the building." *Again* with the hat. "Maybe consider it a welcome home gift, if it makes it easier. It's not finished, in case you don't want it. I built the layout based on researching what other vets have, but we'll get all the rooms set up, counters built, front desk…everything else you'll need once you approve it."

He reaches for his hat, but I step in front of him to stop his hands before he manages to lift it off. As I nudge it back onto his head, his large body decompresses, a load of stress literally rolling off his shoulders.

"You done?"

"Yeah," he breathes, his hand twitching toward his hat again, so I grasp it between mine. "You don't have to accept it. It's a lot, and we never talked about the future or what you're doing next. I don't want you to feel like you have no choices, or like I'm pushing you into this. Don't get me wrong, I *want* you here, but only if you want to be. And—"

I clap my hand over his mouth, ending his nervous rambling, even if it's probably the sweetest thing.

"We haven't talked about my future plans because they include you. You have your business here, and I didn't think too far past that."

He rolls his lips together, dark eyes flicking to the proposed vet office. I won't be able to look at it again without bursting into tears over the fact this man *built* me my business.

He's right; it's a lot. It'll be a huge undertaking, but it's the same way every business in town got built. We all have to start somewhere, and based on what I've been hearing from the residents who come into the diner, many people are desperate for a local vet instead of driving to another town, especially the elderly ones.

"I want to be selfish with you, little rabbit." His hands slide around my waist, keeping me flush against him. "But I also *can't* be selfish when it comes to your happiness. You owned me in high school, and you own me now. It's entirely up to you to decide what to do with me."

My heart bursts with the simple proclamation. With it, I better comprehend the feelings that exist in his presence.

They're not *like.* They're more.

A non-love for a non-friend, except I'm kidding myself on both fronts.

I cup his neck, angling his face down. "Can I keep you?"

"Fuck yes," he breathes, lightning sparking within his stormy eyes.

"Can I love you?"

His hand tangles with my hair, and he tips my head back. "Fuck yes. As long as I can love you, too. Pretty sure I've loved you since I was seventeen-years-old, Payton."

I lift onto my toes, and he takes the invitation, crushing his mouth to mine. It's a kiss of old mistakes and new loves, of past mistakes and future hopes.

Of teenage teasing turned into a profound emotion.

When the kiss ends, I don't go far. "This is the nicest thing anyone's done for me, and the fact you built it yourself makes it even more special. In case it's not obvious, yes, I accept. I love it. Thank you. I can't wait to start this new adventure." My dream, this time not held back by a narcissist.

"You're special, Payton, and I plan on reminding you of that for a long time to come. You and Baker."

"Baker?"

"The bulldog I'll be adopting from the shelter a few towns over. Now that this place will have a vet, I figured it's time to get a pet. After all, I once said I'd bring my dog to you if I had one, and I'll be damned if I'm not your first customer. But first..." He tugs me toward the door, slipping the key into my hand. "Before we get the guys back in here to continue construction, it's only right we christen every wall first."

Key in the lock, excitement thrums through me that this is happening. It's real. Jace comes up behind me, his chest warm against my back, making me shiver. He dips his face into my hair, dragging his nose along my neck.

"I'm happy it was you in the mask."

"Always." His promise rolls down my spine. "No other man will hurt you again. Not while I'm here. As long as you make one vow in return."

My breath catches. "Which is?"

"To always sin with me, little rabbit."

Check out more Twisted Holiday novellas:
Be Mine (Valentine's Day)
Fright Night (Halloween)
Silent Night (Christmas)

Shop signed books by scanning the code below:

ALSO BY M.L. PHILPITT

Fractured Ever Afters

A 6-book (& 2 novellas) mafia romance series of interconnected standalones based on fairytales, featuring the Montreal mafia and the New York Famiglia.

The Desire in Deception (Prequel Novella)

The Hunt in Elusion

The Craving in Slumber

The Beauty in Scars

The Freedom in Captivity

The Sound in Silencea

The Obscurity in Wishing

The Bonds in Christmas (Epilogue Novella)

The Bratva's Elite

A 4-book mafia series of interconnected standalones featuring the Russian Bratva.

Merciless Queen

Deadly Knight

Defensive Rook

Violent Pawn

Captive Writings

A new adult s… …ies that progressively gets darker with …

Ruthless Letters

Obsessive Messages

Vicious Texts

Burning Notes

Twisted Holidays

A series of dark romance holiday novellas

Silent Night

Egg Hunt

Fright Night

Be Mine

Midnight Kiss

Lucky Clover

Black Magick

A 5-book paranormal romance series of interconnected standalones featuring witches, vampires, shifters, mortals, and demons.

Dark Flame

Dark Mist

Dark Storm

Standalones

A Vampire for Christmas

Audiobooks

Silent Night

ABOUT THE AUTHOR

USA Today Bestselling author M.L. Philpitt writes both dark romance and paranormal romance. When she's not writing made-up realities, she's reading them. She lives in Canada with her four pets and survives life with coffee and an obsession with fictional characters, especially the morally grey kind. By day, she masks as a therapist.

WARNINGS

- Mention of past cheating (not between main characters)
- Primal play
- Emotional abuse (not by main character)
- Violence
- Explicit Sexual Content
- Stalking
- Financial abuse (not by main character)
- Attempted Sexual Assault (not by main character)